Don't Give Up the Ghost

THE DELACORTE BOOK OF ORIGINAL GHOST STORIES

Edited by DAVID GALE

Delacorte ▤ Press

Published by
Delacorte Press
Bantam Doubleday Dell Publishing Group, Inc.
1540 Broadway
New York, New York 10036

Book design by Christine Swirnoff

Library of Congress Cataloging in Publication Data

Don't give up the ghost : the Delacorte book of original ghost stories / edited by
David Gale.
p. cm.
Summary: Presents a collection of ghost stories by such authors as Mary
Downing Hahn, Joyce Hansen, and Walter Dean Myers. Includes information
about the authors and their writings.
ISBN 0-385-31109-5
1. Ghost stories, American. 2. Children's stories, American.
[1. Ghosts—Fiction. 2. Short stories.] I. Gale, David, 1955-
II. Title: Do not give up the ghost.
PZ5.D7424 1993
[Fic]—dc20   92-47088   CIP   AC

Manufactured in the United States of America

October 1993

10 9 8 7 6 5 4 3 2 1

BVG

For my parents

CONTENTS

HERE AND NOW

INTRODUCTION

"The bluish glow had stopped at the foot of the bed, where it hovered about four and a half feet off the floor. There seemed to be a shape to it. . . . It was the head of a girl."
—Marion Dane Bauer

"I was gazing upward sleepily when a face appeared suddenly in the rafters above me. It was dead white, thin lipped, with eyes that glistened darkly in the light cast by our dying fire."
—Janet Taylor Lisle

"A rounded, white-haired woman [was] seated on a boulder. The hem of the woman's faded cotton print dress trailed across her sneakers, but her eyes glittered with excitement, and her smile shimmered through the mist."
—Joan Lowery Nixon

Throughout literature, as indeed throughout history, ghost stories have always captured the imagination of writers and readers, storytellers and listeners. The passages quoted above, by three very different writers, show some of the variety of ways that ghosts have been described.

For this collection, as I did for *Funny You Should Ask*, I solicited original short stories from some of the most respected American authors who are currently writing for children and young adults. Here are the results. These twelve ghost stories, in turn chilling, funny, and thought provoking, run the gamut from contemporary to historic and even futuristic; from stories based on traditional motifs to those pulled right from today's headlines. They are a disparate group, but they are all entertaining. And they all share the same key element, a ghost . . . or do they?

The writers whose work appears in this collection are Marion Dane Bauer, Judith Gorog, Constance Greene, Mary Downing Hahn, Joyce Hansen, Johanna Hurwitz, Janet Taylor Lisle, Walter Dean Myers, Theresa Nelson, Joan Lowery Nixon, Barbara Ann Porte, and Gary Soto. All are popular authors whose novels also have been critically acclaimed. Among the honors their books have received are Newbery Honor Book awards; citations as American Library Association Notable Books for Children or Best Books for Young Adults; Coretta Scott King Awards and Honors; Edgar Allan Poe Awards; designations as the best of the year by ALA's *Booklist* or by *School Library Journal;* kudos from *American Bookseller* as a Pick of the Lists; state awards; and honors from child and parent selectors.

You will find some of your favorite authors in this book. This volume may also introduce you to some authors whose work will be new to you. If the stories in this collection whet your appetite, you will be able to find other books by these authors. At the end of each story a short biographical or autobiographical statement will let you know something about the author and his or her writing.

How did this collection come to be? I invited each of the contributors, along with many other authors, to submit a short story for this book. I asked people whose writing I like. Each writer was asked for a ghost story that had never before been published. I looked only at true short stories; excerpts from longer works were not considered. I told the authors that I wanted to present a range of ghost stories, not just traditional forms.

I am grateful for the number of authors who were willing to submit a story, and I want to thank each of them for their generosity in doing so. Unfortunately, I could not accept all of the stories that were submitted, but I am appreciative of the authors' willingness to take part in this project and for giving me the chance to consider their stories. All royalties generated by the sale of this book are being donated to the Association for Library Service to Children (ALSC), a division of the American Library Association, to be applied toward their Distinguished Service to ALSC award.

In this anthology there is a ghost from the future who wants to find out about basketball; two ghosts who are grandmothers—one of whom is not actually haunting her own granddaughter; a ghostly Little Leaguer who sends a message home every year; and ghosts of every size, shape, and description. The stories are loosely grouped into two sections: ghosts from other times, and ghosts in today's world. You don't need to believe in ghosts to enjoy this collection, but see if your feelings toward ghosts don't change by the time you finish the book.

And now, let the haunting begin!

Long Gone or Yet to Come

Give this message to
my parents. . . .

The Last House on Crescent Road

MARY DOWNING HAHN

THE FIRST time I saw him, I was throwing a ball against the school wall. It was a warm summer evening. The sun had already set, and the first stars were coming out, one by one, so slowly you could still count them, but there was enough light to practice pitching and catching.

I was in a pretty bad mood. We'd lost our first game, and it was my fault. First of all, I'd struck out when the bases were loaded. Then, as if that wasn't bad enough, I'd missed an easy fly. When I finally caught up with the ball, I threw it short, and as a result the other team got four runs. By the time we slunk off the field, the score was twelve to five.

"Way to go, Barnes," Travis O'Neil muttered. From the way he was scowling at me it was easy to see who he blamed. Not himself, the champion batter, but me—Adam Barnes, number-one klutz, champion strikeout, all-around jerk.

And it wasn't just Travis who was mad. I got it from everybody. The coach yelled at me, my father yelled at me, Mrs. O'Neil yelled at me. My friends were so mad, they wouldn't even talk to me. Public enemy number one—that's who I was. In the old days I would have been tarred and feathered and run out of Calvertville on a rail.

So here I was all by myself, hurling ball after ball at a brick wall, missing more than I caught, trying not to cry, telling myself people would forget about today. One game —so what? The summer wasn't over, not yet. Surely I'd improve.

Angry at myself, I threw the ball as hard as I could. It came bouncing back, high and fast. I jumped for it, felt it brush my glove and sail on past. When I turned to run after it, there he was, a red-haired boy grinning at me.

"Looking for this?" He hurled the ball straight at me, but instead of trying to catch it I ducked. Like Travis, the boy knew how to throw a ball hard enough to sting your hand right through a glove.

I expected him to laugh. Travis would have, but he just stood there staring at me. He was around my age, eleven or thereabouts, built skinny and short. A total stranger.

"Aren't you going to get the ball?" he asked.

I wheeled around, found it in the tall grass, and turned back to the boy. He was pounding one fist in the palm of a baseball glove, an old one, real leather it looked like. Behind him a bike leaned against its kickstand. It had fat balloon tires, the kind that make no noise. That was probably why I hadn't heard him coming.

"Throw it here," the boy said.

I tossed the ball and he caught it as easy as a frog

4

catches a fly. Barely moved. Just swung his hand out and the ball dropped into his glove. *Plock.*

This time he threw it nice and gentle. When I caught it, he seemed pleased. Back and forth, back and forth, the ball swung through the dusk. Sometimes I missed, sometimes I threw badly and it fell short or went too wide, but most of the time he managed to catch it. He had the same grace Travis had, a way of making every move look easy.

When it was too dark to see the ball, the boy and I sat on the school steps. In the maple near us, locusts buzzed like children repeating lessons, droning on and on monotonously, stopping and starting, stopping and starting.

I glanced at the boy, but he was staring at the maple as if he were trying to calculate its height.

He must have felt me watching him, because he turned to me with an odd question. "How long has that tree been there?"

I did a little mental arithmetic. "About thirty years."

"As long as that?" He looked as if he didn't believe me.

Had I figured wrong? Next to baseball, arithmetic was my worst subject, but thirty years was thirty years. Even a math moron like me could subtract sixty-three from ninety-three and get the right answer.

"My dad's sixth-grade class planted it in 1963," I told him, thinking that might add some credibility to my answer. "It commemorates something, I forget what."

A breeze rustled the maple's leaves, making a sound like girls whispering in the back row. The boy cocked his head and listened for a moment. "What's your name?" he asked.

"Adam Barnes," I said, and he nodded as if I'd given the right answer.

"I'm Charles," he said.

"Are you new in town?"

He shook his head. "I've lived here for some time now."

That surprised me. Calvertville was a small place, and I was sure I'd never seen Charles.

He must have guessed what I was thinking because he added, "I keep to myself."

Before I could think of another question, Charles asked one. "Do you play here every night?"

"I wouldn't call it *play*," I said. "This year my baseball team has a new coach. Mr. Stohl's really tough, he yells at me all the time, says I don't try. I'm always dropping balls, I can't throw straight, I can't hit. Today was our first game and we lost. Everybody said it was my fault."

I glanced at Charles. He was staring at the maple again, but I knew he was listening to me. "I want to get so good, I'll surprise everybody," I told him. "You know, win the game with a great catch or a spectacular home run. Like a kid in a book or a movie . . ."

Scared he'd laugh, I let my voice trail off. It was a dumb idea. Charles had just seen me fumble almost every ball he threw. I was a klutz. He knew it, I knew it, everybody knew it.

To my surprise Charles smiled as if he understood. "You won't learn much bouncing a ball off a wall, Adam."

"I know, but my dad doesn't have time to help me. And my friends think I'm hopeless. This stupid wall is all I have."

"What if I meet you here every night?" Charles asked. "I'm pretty good. I bet I could teach you a lot."

"Do you mean it?"

6

He grinned and hopped on his old Schwinn. "See you tomorrow," he called as he pedaled down Calvert Road. "Same time, same place."

The next evening I got to the school ground before Charles. While I waited for him, I threw a ball against the wall, missing my own throws more often than not. Just as I was about to give up and go home, I saw him pedaling silently toward me, hunched over the handlebars of his Schwinn, his feet whirling. Braking to a stop in a cloud of dust and gravel, he jumped off the bike and let it fall on its side. The noise bounced back to us from the wall. It was the loudest sound I'd ever heard Charles make.

"Sometimes it's hard to get away." He slipped his hand into his glove, and I threw the ball to him.

Back it came, fast and true, but instead of catching it I ducked like I had last night. "Don't throw so hard."

"You're scared it's going to hit you in the face," Charles said, "and break your glasses. Right?"

I nodded. He was absolutely correct.

Tossing his mitt at me, Charles said, "Try this. It's my lucky glove."

It landed in the dirt at my feet. Except for its age the glove looked pretty ordinary. The leather had a mellow smell, a mix of sweat and old shoes and dirt. When I slid my hand inside, it felt soft and warm and slightly damp.

I watched Charles put my glove on. He flexed his fingers and pounded his fist into the palm. "No wonder you can't catch," he said scornfully. "This is a lousy glove."

I shrugged. "Dad says there's no sense wasting money on somebody like me."

7

"Wear mine," Charles said, "and you'll be good, I swear you will."

I bent my fingers like he had and struck my fist against the padding. "They don't make them like this anymore," I said. "How long have you had it?"

"I don't remember." Backing away, Charles spit on the ball and rubbed it between his palms. "Come on," he said, "let's try again. Remember—with my glove on, you can't miss."

I flinched, I shut my eyes, but the ball landed in my cupped glove—*whack*. Closing my other hand over it, I stared at Charles. "I caught it," I yelled, "I caught it."

"Now throw it to me," he shouted. "Come on, don't just stand there gawking! Pretend there's a guy running for home and you have to stop him."

By the time it was dark, I'd caught every ball Charles had thrown. Even the hard ones. Maybe he was right about the glove being lucky. It sure seemed that way. If I could do this well in a game, Travis might actually be impressed, Dad would be pleased, and Mr. Stohl would quit calling me Butterfingers.

As if he read my thoughts, Charles said, "You can keep the glove for a while if you like. I don't need it."

Hugging it to my chest, I leaned toward him. "Why don't you join our team, Charles? You're even better than Travis. Mr. Stohl would give a million bucks to get somebody as good as you."

Without looking at me Charles said, "I wish I could, but I'm not allowed to play anymore. They won't let me."

I waited for him to explain, but instead he got to his feet. "It's late," he said. "I have to go home."

8

Standing under the maple, I watched him ride away. Calvert Road was lined with trees. In the summer their leaves made a shade so dense it was like looking into a tunnel. In seconds the Schwinn was out of sight.

Charles and I played ball together for a couple of weeks. Sometimes we practiced catching and throwing, sometimes we practiced hitting. He knew lots of tricks—how to track the ball with your eyes, when to swing, when to let it go by, how to follow through.

But his biggest trick had nothing to do with baseball. What he was absolutely best at was keeping himself a secret. Who was he? Where did he live? I didn't even know his last name.

"How come I never see you anywhere but here?" I asked him one night.

We were sitting on the school steps, shoulder to shoulder. Even though it was dark, the day's heat lingered, and the air was heavy and still. So still the maple's leaves hung silent and motionless.

Charles glanced at me, but he didn't answer. The streetlight on the corner turned his skin as pale as skimmed milk.

"I'm always looking for you," I went on. "At the swimming pool, the park, the shopping center. What do you do all day? Where do you go?"

"Don't ask so many questions."

Vexed by his secretiveness, I pounded the ball into the glove. *Plock, plock, plock.* Minutes passed. Charles said nothing. He just sat beside me and gazed at the maple.

"I remember when I was taller than that tree," he said suddenly.

"Oh, sure." When he didn't respond to my sarcasm, I added, "Tell me another one, Charles. That tree's a whole lot older than you are."

He looked at me then, and something in his eyes told me to shut up. Uneasily, I edged away from him. Maybe he had problems I didn't know about. Didn't even *want* to know about. A boy who wasn't allowed to join a ball team, a boy who never went anywhere in the daytime.

"Sorry," I mumbled, but I wasn't sure why I was apologizing.

Ignoring me, Charles picked up his bike. Hanging my baseball glove on the handlebar, he said, "I'm not sure I can meet you here again, Adam."

To keep him from leaving I grabbed his arm. "But we have a big game tomorrow," I said. "I was hoping you'd come."

"I wish I could," he said. "You can't imagine how much I'd like to be there."

He started to pedal away, and I ran after him. "What about your glove?"

Charles glanced over his shoulder. "Use it tomorrow," he yelled. "Then take it to my house and give it to my father. Tell him about the game."

He was pedaling faster, vanishing into the black shade of the trees. "But I don't know where you live," I shouted.

"The last house on Crescent Road," he called back. "Ask for Mr. Bradford."

I chased him down Calvert Road. Just ahead, his white shirt glimmered. The reflector on his rear fender gleamed red in a car's headlights. Then he was gone. Just like that. I'd never seen anyone disappear so fast.

Charles would have been proud of me. Not only did I hit a home run when the bases were loaded but I caught a fly at the bottom of the last inning that sewed up the game. Mr. Stohl gave me a bear hug, Travis invited me to his house for pizza, and Dad offered to buy me the best glove he could afford.

"I didn't realize you'd been using such a shabby old thing," he said.

It was a hot afternoon, but as soon as I'd showered and changed my clothes, I walked all the way to Crescent Road by myself. It was on the other side of town, and I was soaked with sweat when I rang the bell. While I waited for someone to open the door, I leaned against the porch railing. The air was sweet with the smell of roses and freshly cut grass. Bees hummed, a bird sang, a cat stalked across the lawn, its eye on a squirrel.

Of Charles there was no sign.

Finally I heard footsteps, sort of slow and shuffly. "All right, all right," someone muttered, "I'm coming."

The door opened, and an old man peered out at me. Scanty white hair, eyes as deep set as a turtle's, bent back, gnarled hands, he looked as if he were expecting me.

"Is Charles here?" I asked.

The old man shook his head. "I'm Mr. Bradford," he said. "Charles's father."

Before I could tell him why I'd come, Mr. Bradford said, "You've brought his glove, haven't you?"

I held it toward him. "Charles told me to give it to you,"

11

I said. "I was hoping he'd be home to hear about the game."

Mr. Bradford took the glove and cradled it as if it were a newborn baby. "The bases were loaded and you hit a home run," he said. "Then, at the bottom of the last inning, you caught the fly that won the game."

I stared at him. "How did you know?"

Mr. Bradford opened the door wider and stepped aside to let me in. For the first time I noticed the old woman behind him. When I realized she was crying, I edged away, but she reached out and took my hand.

"Please come with me," she said softly.

Too embarrassed to protest, I followed her upstairs to a small room at the end of the hall. The late-afternoon sunlight slanted through the windows and sparkled on a row of trophies. The walls were covered with pictures of old-timers like Hank Aaron and Sandy Koufax. A faded Baltimore Orioles pennant hung over a neatly made bed. Several cigar boxes full of baseball cards sat on the bureau next to a stack of comic books.

Outside, a lawn mower sputtered, a dog barked, an airplane droned. Ordinary summer noises—but for some reason they didn't sound right. In Charles's silent room I felt like an archaeologist looking at things untouched for centuries.

Squeezing my hand, Mrs. Bradford said, "You're not the first boy to bring my son's glove home."

Despite the heat a shiver ran up and down my spine. "What do you mean?"

Mr. and Mrs. Bradford gazed at each other. "The telling's so hard," the old woman said.

"It doesn't get easier no matter how often we explain," her husband agreed. "But you do it best," he added.

I looked from one to the other. Mrs. Bradford wiped her eyes and took a deep breath. "Thirty years ago today Charles hit a home run when the bases were loaded. At the bottom of the last inning he caught the fly that won the game."

She paused and glanced at her husband, but he had his back to us. "Charles came rushing home on his bike, fast and reckless, too excited to be careful."

Her voice faltered and Mr. Bradford put his arm around his wife's shoulders. "Before he got here, a car hit him in front of the elementary school," he said. "Even though he couldn't tell us himself, he sends a boy home every now and then with the news—and his glove."

"Are you saying Charles is dead?" I whispered.

"You don't believe us," Mrs. Bradford said. "No one ever does."

I backed away from them one step at a time, finding the stairs with my feet like a blind man. My knees were so weak, I thought I'd fall. It was a trick, I told myself, a hoax Charles had dreamed up and talked his parents into sharing.

Mr. Bradford followed me to the door. "Go to the school," he said. "There's a maple by the front steps. Read the bronze plaque."

Without saying good-bye I ran across the neatly trimmed lawn and dashed up Crescent Road without looking back. At first my only thought was to go home, but as I passed the school I saw my baseball glove hanging from a branch on the maple. That Charles—what a weird sense of humor he had. Boy, would he laugh when he found out I'd almost fallen for his joke.

Convinced he was hiding behind the tree, I called him. My voice bounced back from the school's wall. The only other sound was the cooing of a mourning dove.

"Where are you, Charles?" I circled the maple, but there was no sign of him. "Quit fooling around, darn it. Come on out."

Fed up with Charles's tricks, I grabbed my glove from the limb, but it was so cold, it slipped from my fingers and landed in the tall grass. When I reached for it, I saw the bronze plaque.

Remembering what Mr. Bradford had said, I felt my throat tighten. I'd noticed the plaque before, but I'd never bothered to look at the inscription. It was from long ago, I'd thought, way back when my parents were kids. Nothing to do with me. Now I knelt down and smoothed the grass away.

IN MEMORY OF OUR BELOVED CLASSMATE, CHARLES ROBERT BRADFORD, I read. 8 MARCH 1952–17 JULY 1963.

As I stared at the words, a shadow fell across the plaque. "Here you are, Adam. I've been looking for you."

Startled by my father's voice, I scrambled to my feet. Pointing at the plaque, I said, "He died thirty years ago today."

"Charlie Bradford," Dad said softly. "He was the best ballplayer in Calvertville. If he'd lived, he'd have been a pro today."

Turning to me, he added, "You reminded me of him this afternoon, Adam. The way you hit that homer—straight across the creek just like he used to. And the fly you caught. You were Charlie all over again. The champ."

To hide my tears I threw my arms around Dad and hugged him hard. We stayed like that for a while. It was just about the closest we'd ever been, and neither one of us wanted to pull away.

Before we left the playground, I looked back. For a moment I thought I saw Charles leaning against the maple's trunk, but it must have been a trick of light. When I stared hard, he vanished.

"We'll get a new glove tomorrow," Dad said. "Real leather. This vinyl feels as cold as a dead man's hand."

He tossed the glove into a trash can and slung his arm around my shoulders. We walked home that way, slow and easy, watching the stars come out one by one.

About Mary Downing Hahn

Until recently I was a children's librarian. When I visited schools to book-talk, I soon realized that my favorite novels were often far above the kids' reading level. To avoid frustrating them with the old line "If you want to know what happens next visit the library and ask for this book," I always told them at least one story from start to finish. To be sure of holding their interest I usually chose it from an anthology such as Alvin Schwartz's *Scary Stories to Tell in the Dark* or Maria Leach's *The Thing at the Foot of the Bed*.

Among my favorites were "Wait Till Martin Comes" (which gave me the title for one of my books) and "The Phantom Hitchhiker." When I was asked to contribute to this anthology, I decided to write a variant of the hitchhiker story.

Now I visit schools as a writer and talk about my own books. I'm frequently asked where I get my ideas. Although I'm sometimes tempted to make up silly sources, I tell kids my stories are a combination of fact and fiction. Like most writers I often begin with something that really happened (or might have happened or almost happened or should have happened) and expand upon it by asking the famous what-if question: What if the dead man in the woods was murdered? What if the graveyard was haunted? What if the doll in the garden was stolen? What if that weird old woman was a witch?

Of my twelve books only two are ghost stories, but they are the ones children most often want to know about. "Did you ever see a ghost?" "Do you believe in ghosts?" "Why do you write about ghosts?"

Unfortunately, I've never encountered a ghost, but I've read many supposedly true accounts of "gray ladies" who vanish through walls and "gentlemen dressed in brown" who appear

16

unexpectedly at the door. Who am I to doubt the veracity of these stories?

As for writing about the supernatural—quite simply, the subject intrigues me.

Someone is listening. . . .

Sweet Hour of Prayer

JOYCE HANSEN

ALL OF my life I'd heard stories that Cracke Road was haunted. The road was once part of a plantation in Charleston, South Carolina, back in slavery times and was rumored to be haunted by the spirits of people who had run away from slavery and the plantation.

It was said that on dark moonless nights, these spirits could be seen slipping behind the oaks and magnolias that lined the road. People claimed that the ghosts were always spotted traveling in a northerly direction.

Everybody who lived on the road had a ghost story to tell—except my family. My mother would say to me, "Those stories are nothing but a bunch of silly tales people are making up to entertain themselves."

I didn't believe the stories, either, until Lillian came to live on Cracke Road. I first saw her on a late summer afternoon as I sat on my porch shelling butter beans with my mother. I lived at the end of Cracke Road, where nothing exciting ever happened. Our only nearby neighbors were Miss Mary and her husband, Mr. Ross, who lived in the house across the road from us. I was ten years old and had known Miss Mary and Mr. Ross all of my life and had never seen them smile.

My friend Junie and her family lived at the other end of the road—the fun end where there was light and laughter. Junie called my end of the road the cemetery because it was a dead end.

That summer afternoon I glanced up the road and saw a girl my age and a woman walking toward us. The girl, sobbing pitifully, clutched a doll in one hand and the woman's arm in the other.

Both Mama and I looked, but I guess I stared too hard.

"Mind your business," Mama whispered to me, and went back to shelling beans. They had to be going to visit the Rosses, since we didn't know them. A new face on Cracke Road was always an interesting event. I continued to stare.

When they turned into the Rosses' pathway I said, "No wonder that girl is crying. Who would want to visit Miss Mary and Mr. Ross?"

"Marilyn, I told you not to talk about Miss Mary and her husband—you're just a child." In 1930 children were not allowed to have opinions about their elders. Poor girl, I thought. But why was she crying so hard? I wondered. A visit didn't *really* last forever.

"The four-o'clocks are open now," my mother said. "I'll finish the beans."

I jumped off the porch and picked the purple blossoms of the four-o'clocks.

As I gathered the flowers, the woman, who I guessed was the girl's mother, left the house without her daughter. Her eyes looked sorrowful.

"That's why she was crying so hard," I said, without stopping to think about whose business I was minding.

My mother, being as nosy as I was, forgot to chastise me. "Well, Miss Mary must be caring for that child for a spell." Mama stood up. "It's no business of ours. But now you'll have someone on this end of the road to play with." My mother went in the house and I watched the slender woman walk quickly up the road. "Come on in, Marilyn," Mama called from the window. "Your daddy will be home soon."

I cleaned the kitchen table and set out the dishes, all the while peeping out of my kitchen window, which faced the Rosses' house. There was nothing different over there—a dim light behind the lace curtains, two wicker rocking chairs side by side on the Rosses' porch, and several flower pots resting on the porch's railing. I looked toward the dead end and the large oak tree with gray moss hanging like drapes from its branches. Everything was as usual.

After dinner I cleaned the table and helped Mama wash the dishes. I then took my jar for catching fireflies off the shelf over the kitchen sink and made sure that I had a couple of pieces of string in my skirt pocket.

"Mama, I'm going to make friends with the new girl, then I'll take her up the road to meet Junie and them."

"Okay, but she looks like a quiet child to me. She might not like Junie."

When I went outside, Miss Mary and Mr. Ross sat in their rocking chairs as they did every evening. The girl, holding her doll to her heart and her head down, sat on the porch steps. I crossed the road and stepped up to the Rosses' porch.

"Evening, Miss Mary, Mr. Ross," I said, smiling at the top of the girl's head.

"Evening," they both responded at the same time, watching me suspiciously.

"Hello," I said to the girl. "My name is Marilyn. What's yours?"

"Lillian," she whispered, looking up at me with the same sorrowful brown eyes as her mother's.

"Can Lillian come up the road with me to play with Junie?" I asked.

They stopped rocking. Mr. Ross grunted. "No," Miss Mary answered, glaring at me. "Mr. Ross and I are responsible for her. Junie and them ain't nothing but a bunch of ruffians. I don't know why your mother allows you to play with them."

I hid my anger. There was nothing wrong with Junie and the rest of them. They were just a little poorer than we were. I could faintly hear Big Bob's guitar. Mr. Ross rocked a little faster in his chair and began to sing a spiritual, drowning out Bob's blues.

"You-all stay right here at this end of the road," Miss Mary said, and then joined her husband in song. Every night when they sat outside they'd sing old spirituals. It was their way of praying, my mother had told me.

"Go in the wilderness,
  Go in the wilderness,
  Go in the wilderness,"

21

they sang, and I felt uneasy, as I always did when I heard those slavery-time spirituals. That's why I liked to be up the road with Junie when the Rosses started their singing. I held out my empty jar. "Want to catch fireflies?" I asked Lillian.

She shook her head.

"Then I'll show you how to make a necklace out of the four-o'clocks if you don't already know."

She didn't answer but followed me to my porch and sat silently while I pulled a piece of string through the blossoms, making necklaces for her and her doll. The sun had set and the crickets and frogs added their voices to the Rosses' spirituals. I tried to ignore their singing and the way the song seemed to bring deep shadows, especially where the road ended and the large oak tree stood like a guard at the dead end.

When I finished the necklaces, I decided to fill my jar with fireflies. I held the top of the jar slightly open and snapped them up. I'd pretend that they were tiny gold nuggets and imagine all the wonderful things I'd buy with them. When the jar was full I returned to the porch and held the jar up for Lillian to admire, but I could tell that her thoughts were somewhere else.

"When's your mother coming back for you?" I asked.

She shrugged her shoulders and kept staring at the ground.

"She'll be back soon, won't she?" I asked hopefully.

Lillian finally looked at me, tears brimming on her eyelids. "My mother had to go to New York so she could work. I have to stay with Miss Mary and Mr. Ross until she sends for me. We used to have a lot of fun together." Lillian stared lovingly at the doll. "She gave me this doll before she left."

I'd always lived with my own family and couldn't imagine what I'd do if they had to leave me with Miss Ross and her husband. I suddenly wanted to be with Junie and them, but I couldn't leave Lillian. If anyone needed a friend, she did.

The Rosses started singing

"Sweet hour of prayer,
Sweet hour of prayer
That brought me from a world of care
Meet me at my father's throne
And make my wants and wishes known . . ."

The screen door squeaked and Mama came out with a pitcher of lemonade. It tasted sweet and cool on that sweltering summer night.

As we drank our lemonade, Miss Mary and her husband finished singing. "Lillian," Miss Mary called. Lillian thanked my mother, walked slowly across the road, and disappeared inside the house. I could hear the radio coming from the living room, where my father sat, and Big Bob's guitar drifting down from Junie's end of the road.

My mother sat on the steps next to me as I freed the fireflies. "She seems to be a nice girl."

I told her about Lillian. She took a long swallow of lemonade. "It's too bad her mother had to leave her," she said, "but I'm sure she'll send for her when she's able to."

The next morning I expected to see Lillian outside so we could play with our dolls. I never called on Miss Mary except if my mother sent me there to borrow some sugar or flour. I was a little nervous as I shouted through the screen door. "Morning, Miss Mary. Can Lillian come to my house?"

Miss Mary came to the screen door, wiping her hands on her flowered apron.

"She's busy."

"Can she come out when she's finished, ma'am?" I asked.

"Maybe."

She left me standing there.

I went back home and Mama was making iced tea. "I thought that you were going to invite Lillian over here."

"Miss Mary says she can't come out. Why is she so mean?"

"I told you about being disrespectful to your elders. Miss Mary's not mean. She never had any children of her own, so she's a little strict, but she's a good God-fearing woman."

I didn't see Lillian until the evening after supper. She sat on the porch steps, still holding on to the beautiful brown doll. This time, however, she smiled when she saw me. The Rosses were seated in their rockers. "Can I play with Marilyn?" Lillian asked.

I was surprised that she spoke up.

Miss Mary nodded. "Long as you stay on this end of the road."

Lillian rested her doll on the porch steps and I handed her an empty jar so that we could catch fireflies together. Miss Mary and Mr. Ross began to sing. Lillian caught more fireflies than I did.

"Here, take some of mine," she offered when we plopped down on the bench under the oak tree. Usually, I didn't play near the very end of the road at night when I was alone. The dead end was only a few feet away from the two houses, but it was scary to me because on a moonless night the open field beyond looked like the very edge of the world. In the daytime it was just a field.

But on the night that Lillian and I chased fireflies, the moon was full and bright and the kerosene lamps from our houses cast a warm dark golden glow on us.

"Look, Marilyn," Lillian said, holding up the jar, "they're sparkling like tiny lamps." Suddenly she looked sad. "My mother and I used to catch fireflies. She'd say that they were tiny chips of sunlight."

"Sweet hour of prayer, sweet hour of prayer that brought me from a world of care . . ." Miss Mary and Mr. Ross sang. Deep shadows seemed to suddenly dim our light, and I was frightened. "Let's go back to my porch," I said, dashing away from the shadows. We sat on my porch, admiring our fireflies and then freeing them when my mother came out with a pitcher of ice tea and a plate of ginger snaps for us.

"Lillian," Miss Mary called.

"Can you come out early tomorrow?" I asked her.

"Miss Mary says I can't just eat, sleep, and play. I have to help with chores." Then she ran across the road. Mr. Ross got up and walked stiffly into the house, while Miss Mary straightened the rockers.

Suddenly Lillian turned around and dashed back to our side of the road. "My doll. Did you see it?"

"You left it on the porch," I said.

"No one would take it," my mother said. "Go check the porch again, sweetie, it has to be there."

Tears rolled down Lillian's face and she ran back across the road. I felt sorry for her. "Go on, help her find the doll," my mother said.

I stepped up boldly onto the porch. I even had the nerve to look under the pillows on Miss Mary's rocking chairs. We searched behind the stack of firewood and several empty flower pots. No doll.

The screen door opened. "What're you children doing?"

"I can't find my doll," Lillian sobbed.

"You need to learn how to take better care of your things. Go in the house."

My father was still listening to the radio when I followed my mother inside the house. "Miss Mary probably picked that doll up and brought it inside. It'll turn up," my mother said.

The next morning I saw Miss Mary walking down the road, carrying an umbrella over her head to protect herself from the sun. Mr. Ross was long gone to his shrimp boat. Lillian wasn't outside. I called through the screen door. She came to the door with a broom in her hand and big sorrowful eyes.

"Did you find your doll?"

She shook her head, "No."

"Can you come to my house and play? I'll give you one of my dolls. But they're not as pretty as yours."

"I have to clean the kitchen, then I have to pick the okra out of the backyard."

"I'll help you."

"Miss Mary said I can't have company."

That evening when I went outside, Lillian wasn't there yet. I picked the four-o'clocks to make necklaces for the dolls so that they wouldn't look so tacky. I heard through her open kitchen window Miss Mary singing. "Sweet hour, of prayer, in season of distress and grief, my soul has often found relief . . ." she sang. I was busy twining the necklaces when Lillian ran down the steps with a wide smile on her face. She raced over to me.

"You found your doll?"

"Yes."

"Where was it?"

"Up in the attic in a trunk where Miss Mary hid it."

"How did you find it?"

"The girl told me."

"What girl?"

"The girl who used to live here."

"No girl ever lived with Miss Mary. I would have known her."

Lillian talked so softly, I could hardly hear her. "It was a long time ago when all of this land was a plantation. The girl was a slave."

"Miss Mary's been telling you them old Cracke Road ghost stories."

"Miss Mary doesn't tell me stories." Her face brightened. "My mother used to tell me stories. Wonderful stories."

"How did the girl look?"

"She had two thick braids that touched her shoulders

and wore one of those long, old-fashioned gingham dresses."

I looked in Lillian's mouth to see whether she had a gap in her two front teeth, which meant that a person was a liar. Her front teeth were closed and straight.

"Are you lying, Lillian?"

"No. She led me to where the doll is and she is going to help me get to my mama."

"But your mother is all the way in New York."

"The girl told me that she had escaped from slavery in 1863."

"You talked to a ghost?"

"Yes."

"You weren't afraid?"

"No, she's very nice. Whenever I want to see her, I sing 'Sweet Hour of Prayer' or 'Go in the Wilderness.' "

Nobody else ever said in their ghost stories that they spoke to the spirit. I thought that maybe Lillian was a little "teched" in the head, as the old people used to say. In other words, she was crazy.

Lillian smiled and her eyes shone. "The girl said she would help me run away to my mother. She said that when she escaped from the plantation, those same songs Mr. Ross and Miss Mary sing now were signals the slaves used back then when they made plans to meet somewhere or run away."

I peeped at the oak tree and the dead end. "Where is the girl now?"

Lillian shrugged. "I don't know. But she also told me that the night they all left the plantation, the signal that it was safe to leave was when some of the people who were

too old or sick to run away sang 'Sweet Hour of Prayer.' "
Lillian pointed to the oak.

"The girl said she hid behind that tree with her mother
and when the old people sang, she and the other runaways
took off and headed north."

Only the light from the kerosene lamps lit our end of
the road. I didn't know what to believe. Maybe Lillian just
liked to make up stories. "I don't believe in ghosts," I said.
"I think you just made all of that up."

"But I didn't," she insisted. "There is a girl who told me
all of this. She was in the house with me and showed me
where the doll was."

"Did Miss Mary see her?"

"No. Miss Mary was in the kitchen singing, like she does
sometime when she's cooking."

"Where does this girl live now? And if she ran away, why
is she back here?"

Lillian folded her arms. "I guess she lives wherever spirits do and she can come back whenever she pleases." She
reached for one of my dolls. "Can I play with your doll?
Can't let Miss Mary find out that I know where my doll is.
I'll take her back when I leave with the girl."

I handed her a doll. But the ghost talk was making me
nervous.

"Sweet hour of prayer, sweet hour of prayer,
    That brought me from a world of care . . ."

Miss Mary and Mr. Ross sang from the porch.

I felt as if someone were there watching me and Lillian.

I jumped off the porch step. "I'm going up to Junie and them," I said, and dashed up Cracke Road as fast as I could.

Big Bob's blues drowned out "Sweet Hour of Prayer."

The men sat in front of the grocery store like they did every summer night after work. Junie and the other kids played tag. I ripped and roared with them until my mother called me home. As I ran back to my end of the road I felt ashamed for leaving Lillian. I realized that I'd only imagined someone was watching us because of Lillian's story. Lillian was still sitting on the bench under the oak, playing with my dolls.

"Hi, Marilyn." She waved and seemed so happy. She stood up and handed me the dolls. "Thank you," she said, and followed Mr. Ross and Miss Mary into the house without waiting for them to call her. I was glad that she wasn't angry with me for leaving her.

The next day I didn't look for Lillian, since she couldn't come out anyway and I didn't want to hear about ghosts. I picked peaches with Junie and spent the rest of the afternoon on her end of the road. While me and Junie sat on her porch and ate peaches, I saw my mother and Miss Mary walking quickly toward us and I knew something was wrong. "Is Lillian up here with you?" my mother asked excitedly.

"No," I said.

Miss Mary wrung her hands. "That's why I don't like to be responsible for other people's children."

"Seems like Lillian ran away," my mother said.

I couldn't believe it.

"Did she say anything to you?" Mama asked me.

I hesitated. Who would believe what Lillian had told me?

30

"Well?" My mother put her face in mine. "What did she say?"

"She said the spirit of a girl who used to live here was going to help her get to her mother."

Miss Mary put her hands on her hips. "Did the girl also tell her to go in my attic and take that doll which I was just keeping safe for her since she was so careless with it?"

"Yes, ma'am, she said that the girl told her where the doll was."

Junie and them crowded around us, soaking up every word.

My mother grabbed my arm.

"Marilyn, come on home. This is no time for playing." She turned to Junie and them. "If you see a little girl named Lillian, let me or Miss Mary know."

Miss Mary threw her head up in the air and started back down the road. Me and my mother followed.

I told them everything. Miss Mary narrowed her eyes as she stared at me. "Your mother needs to give you a decent beating for telling them foolish ghost stories."

"I'm telling you what Lillian told me," I protested.

My mother turned to Miss Mary. "Maybe Lillian has an overactive imagination, Miss Mary. You know children do make up imaginary friends—especially lonely children."

Miss Mary folded her arms. "She didn't hear those stories from me. But I'm remembering something now." She sat down on our porch steps. "My grandmother was born into slavery. And she had a sister who escaped from this very same area when it was a plantation. And the slaves used to sing spirituals as secret codes and messages when they were making plans to escape." Miss Mary turned to

31

me. "You say the ghost comes when we sing the spirituals?"

"Yes, ma'am."

My mother looked confused. "You didn't tell Lillian that story?" she asked.

"Absolutely not. I forgot it myself, until just now."

Mama stood up. "Well, it's just a coincidence. Lillian will come back when she gets hungry and tired. In the meantime we'll help you find her. How far can a little girl go by herself? She's just missing her mama, that's all."

I felt awful and wished I'd been a better friend to Lillian. Maybe she wouldn't have run away then. There was a big search on for Lillian. Everyone who lived on Cracke Road looked for her. When my father came in from work he joined Big Bob and the other men in the search. No Lillian.

When the men returned from combing through the city and nearby woods Daddy sat with my mother and me on the porch.

"This is a mystery." My mother fanned herself.

"It's no mystery. The child just ran away is all," my father said. "Miss Mary probably forgot that she told her that story," he added.

I gazed over at the Rosses' house. Though my parents didn't say so, I knew that they were waiting, like I was, for Miss Mary and Mr. Ross to come out and sing their spirituals so that we could see the spirits in the dark. My father rarely sat outside with us in the evenings.

The crickets and frogs and Big Bob's guitar made their night music. The stars filled the sky, but Miss Mary and Mr. Ross did not come outside that night.

My mother poured herself a glass of lemonade. "Guess they must be upset about that child. But you know, I got used to hearing them sing every night. I miss it."

I was disappointed too. Since I was sitting safely between my mother and father, I wasn't afraid to see this spirit.

"Do you and Daddy know the words to 'Sweet Hour of Prayer'?" I asked.

"Of course," my mother answered. "Your father and I have been singing that spiritual every Sunday since we were children."

She began to sing.

"Sweet hour of prayer,
   Sweet hour of prayer
   that brought me from a world of care . . ."

My father joined her.

"Meet me at my father's throne
   And make my wants and wishes known . . ."

Then I joined them, because I'd heard the spiritual so much I knew the words by heart too. And as we sang together I did not feel uneasy or afraid as I used to.

"In seasons of distress and grief
   My soul has often found relief
   And oft escaped the tempter's snare
   By thy re—"

I leapt off the step and pointed toward the oak tree. "Look! There she is!"

"Who?" My mother craned her neck. "Lillian?"

My father stood up quickly. "You-all didn't see anything. Just the power of suggestion. I'm going in to listen to Fats Waller on the radio."

My mother stood up and nervously wiped her hands on her dress. "We're getting just like these other foolish folks round here, conjuring up ghosts. Come on, Marilyn, let's make some more lemonade. Sure is hot tonight."

I followed my mother and father into the house and said no more about the ghost. But I knew on that summer night that I had seen a girl, with two thick braids touching her shoulders, wearing a long gingham dress, slip behind the oak tree. I knew my parents had seen her, too, but they didn't want to believe what they'd seen.

Miss Mary and Mr. Ross went to the police the next day.

"Children run away all the time," one of the policemen told them. "That little gal is probably okay."

The people on Cracke Road, however, continued to search for Lillian for the rest of the week. But there was no trace of her.

I knew that Lillian wouldn't be found in South Carolina and I was the only one who wasn't surprised when two weeks later her mother wrote Miss Mary a letter saying that Lillian was safe and sound with her in New York City.

People were shocked. "It's amazing—it's unbelievable—how did that little girl get all the way to big New York City by herself?" they exclaimed. I knew how.

I never saw Lillian or the ghost again, and since that summer in 1930 I have moved far away from Cracke Road. But now in my old age I, too, sing the old spirituals and feel the kindly spirits of my ancestors watching over me.

About Joyce Hansen

This story was inspired by an event in my mother's childhood. In 1922 her family had to leave Charleston, South Carolina, to find work in the North. My mother, Lillian, was left in the care of an elderly, strict childless couple who sat on their porch every evening singing hymns and spirituals (religious songs created by enslaved Africans in the United States). My mother has often said that certain spirituals always remind her of those lonely, frightening days.

Her most treasured possession at this time was a beautiful black doll her brother had given her. One day she left the doll on the porch and it was gone when she returned. She was devastated, grieving for her mother and her lost doll. Her story has a happy ending: She joined her mother in New York and the woman who cared for her had put the doll away for safekeeping and returned it to her the day Lillian left South Carolina.

I had wanted to tell this story but had no idea what form it would take, until I began to think about the importance of the spirituals in understanding African-American culture. During slavery runaways would often sing spirituals as a way of sending secret messages to one another. I chose the spiritual "Sweet Hour of Prayer" because it is one of my favorites. It has a slow, haunting melody with words that offer comfort in the face of stress and pain.

I have written six books for young people and was the recipient of the Coretta Scott King Honor Book Award in 1987. My latest book is *Between Two Fires,* a nonfiction book about black soldiers in the Civil War. I presently teach creative writing at Charles R. Drew Intermediate school in The Bronx, New York City.

*A ghost from the future learns about
the religion of Hoops. . . .*

Things That Go Gleep in the Night

WALTER DEAN MYERS

K EVIN BATTLE poured a glass of orange juice with one hand while he pushed the buttons on the television remote with the other. The picture on the screen broke into a thousand diagonal pieces and the sound crackled noisily. The next channel was no better. He started to put the juice back into the refrigerator, noticed that there were Fig Newtons on the shelf, and grabbed a handful. He flicked the power switch on the remote to "off" and watched as the brightly colored patterns first faded and then shrank. He would watch television in his room, he thought.

He checked the time—three-fifteen. He'd start his math homework at five-fifteen so he'd be halfway through it by the time his mother got home at six.

He hadn't remembered leaving the light on in his room, but he saw the glow coming from the door as he reached the second floor of the Battle household. Maybe his mother had been in his room after he had left for school, he thought. He pushed the door open with his foot as he tried to remember how he had left the room. Messy enough, he knew, to get a lecture about neatness.

Inside the room he froze. The overhead light wasn't on and yet the room was bathed in an eerie green light. In the mirror over his dresser he could see his closet. The door was partially open and he saw that the glow came from within. He eased the orange juice and Fig Newtons down on his dresser, took a deep breath, and held it for a long moment before speaking.

"Hello?"

"Hello?" a voice answered. The green glow began to fade.

"Hey, Jimmy, is that you fooling around?" Kevin remembered that he hadn't seen his best friend on the school bus.

"Kevin Battle?" The voice from the closet spoke softly as the door opened. "Are you really Kevin Battle?"

Kevin jumped back, one hand flat against the wall of his room, as a pale, thin figure emerged from the closet. Kevin would have run if there hadn't been something vaguely familiar about what clearly looked to be a youngish, if odd-looking, man. He was dressed strangely. The white tunic he wore came down nearly to his knees, and his sandals were strapped over his ankles so that they looked almost like boots.

"I'm Kevin Battle." Kevin felt a cold trickle of sweat down the back of his neck. "Who are you?"

38

"I'm Orion Battle." The quick answer was accompanied by a smile. "And I'm thrilled and honored to meet you."

"Orion Battle?" Kevin didn't move from the door. "You stay right there. And how did you get in here in the first place?"

"It's kind of a long story," he said. "I'd love to tell you if you'll just give me a chance. And don't worry, I won't say gleep or anything."

"Gleep?"

"That's what some people think ghosts do"—Orion Battle sat on the edge of Kevin's bed—"go around sneaking up on people and saying gleep!"

"Ghosts?"

"I'm from a long time from now," Orion said. "The year 3003, to be exact. And technically I'm not alive, so I imagine you'd call me a ghost."

"And ghosts go gleep?" Kevin looked at him. "Whatever happened to boo!"

"Boo?"

"Forget it," Kevin said. "I don't believe a word of what you're saying."

"I was sure you'd have trouble understanding," Orion said. "But I was also pretty sure a man as wise as you would listen to me."

"Yeah, maybe." Kevin relaxed slightly. "Go ahead."

"Well, a while back, I think it was 2500, something like that—"

"A while back?"

"From my point of view," Orion added quickly. "Anyway, around that time we finally conquered death. Found out that it was a virus. But people still had to be—you

39

know—moved out of the way so new people could be born. So we started doing it by lottery."

"You mean, so you picked a number and you were killed?" Kevin asked.

"Not exactly," Orion said. "I've just been deenergized. I'll become part of some other form, perhaps even another person. So nobody ever 'dies' the way they used to in your time. But a really neat thing that we have, is that after we get deenergized we can travel in time for a short while before we lose consciousness and start the transference part."

"Yeah?"

"And since I had the chance," Orion said, "here I am."

"So let's get this straight," Kevin said. "You're a ghost from the future, and you decided to come here to see me before you just kind of float away into random energy?"

"Yeah, I knew you'd get it," Orion said. "I mean, with your wisdom and all. Can you imagine how proud I am of having you for an ancestor?"

"I'm your ancestor?" Kevin asked.

"According to the records we could find," Orion said. "You're my great-great-great-great-great-great-great-great-great-grandfather. You're also one of the most famous men in this century. Well, I guess you're going to be. We're still quoting your wisdom in the year 3003."

"Like what wise sayings?" Kevin took a sip from his orange juice.

"My personal favorite was when you said that Truth is circular and that life goes in a straight line, which was the basic cause of human confusion."

"Yeah, that's uh . . . what I've been thinking about a lot," Kevin said.

"It took me a while to understand it," Orion said. "But when I did, it was just wonderful."

"Glad you liked it, Orion," Kevin said. "It is Orion?"

"Yes, that's right. Anyway, when my number came up I thought I'd take the chance to meet you." Orion stood and started stretching his hands over his head and touching his toes. "And find out about one of the minor religions in your time that nobody in our time could really figure out."

"What minor religion?" Kevin wondered if this guy was some kind of nut. "And what are you doing?"

"Oh, circulation exercises," Orion said. "In our time we don't do much in the way of physical activities. Got to save the old oxygen, you know."

"You people have problems with the atmosphere?"

"Not since the domes were built," Orion said. "We manufacture as much as oxygen as we need, but we can't use it too quickly. It gets too expensive."

"And what religion do you want to know about?" Kevin asked.

"There's some controversy about what you people call it." Orion stopped exercising and cupped his chin in his hand. "Some of our archaeologists think you called it B-Ball and some think you called it Hoops—"

"B-Ball? Hoops?" Kevin scratched his head. "We've got a lot to talk about, friend."

"Uh—what shall I call you? Grandpa?"

"Sure, why not," Kevin said.

"Look, Grandpa, I don't have a lot of time here. I'll be

deenergizing in an hour or so. So if you explain it to me in a quick way, I would appreciate it."

"Okay, let me get this straight. You guys in the future don't do many physical things, right?"

"We don't do anything physical, really," Orion said.

"And you don't know anything about our 'religion' of Hoops?"

"Well, we know some things," Orion said. "We know there were two goals. One that is Good and the other Evil. You had people who were magicians and others who could fly through the air."

"And you still quote my wisdom?"

"Yes, I'm proud to say." Orion beamed. "How old are you now?"

"Fourteen," Kevin said.

"Then you have just started saying your wise things," Orion said.

"Okay, look, I'm going to show you some of our 'hoops,' " Kevin said.

"I'd be honored," Orion replied.

Kevin took the phone. He punched the number he wanted with one hand and flicked on the television with the other. "You people still use televisions?"

Orion looked at the television and nodded. "We call it 'Vision.' "

"Vision?" Kevin was amazed. "After a thousand years you just call it vision? That's it? Do you have holographic vision?"

"What's that?" Orion asked.

"Hello, Jimmy?" Kevin spoke into the phone. "Look, I want to get up a three-man run. You up to it?"

"Yeah, I guess so." Jimmy's voice seemed far away on the phone. "Who we going to play against?"

"Call up Eddie Farrell, and Billy Garcia, see if he can get his brother and Sean Harmon."

"You got to be kidding. Sean Harmon can dunk backwards!" Jimmy said.

"Don't sweat it, Jimmy," Kevin said. "I know what I'm doing. I mean, I am a little wiser than you. I'll meet you in the gym in twenty minutes."

"Yeah, right," Jimmy said. "We're going to get killed and you're talking about how wise you are."

It was a short walk to the gym, but Kevin had to walk slowly. In the first place Orion was out of breath after the first half block, and then he had to stop to see everything.

"It's really wild that you guys have oxygen that's just floating around and doesn't even need a dome to keep it in," Orion said.

"Well, we're trying our best to keep it," Kevin said. "At least some of us are."

"I think that's a wise thing too," Orion said. "You really are wise."

"What's the wisest thing you know I've said?" Kevin asked.

"Oh, that thing about the end of Truth being the beginning of oppression," Orion said. "That's my personal favorite."

"I can understand that," Kevin said.

"And tell me, were you the one who discovered that by adding microbes to the garbage dumps you would have a source of perpetual energy?"

"I've been thinking about it," said Kevin.

"Fantastic!"

They reached the basketball court just as Jimmy arrived with Eddie.

"Sean and the Garcia brothers were already here," Jimmy said. "Who's this guy?"

"Hello, my name is Orion. I'm Kevin's—"

"Friend," Kevin added quickly.

"That's a truly funky outfit, man," Jimmy said. "You get it at the mall?"

"No," Kevin said quickly. "It's kind of homemade."

Kevin found a seat for Orion. "You're in for a treat," he said. "Harmon is like the best ever."

"I'll be respectful," Orion said.

"And we're only going to use one goal," Kevin said. "It's three on three."

"Is it the goal of Good or the goal of Evil?" Orion asked.

"Who knows?" Kevin shrugged as he tightened the laces on his sneakers.

"It's the search for truth?" Orion asked.

"Yeah, something like that," Kevin said.

The game started just about as Jimmy thought it would.

Juan Garcia, the shorter of the Garcia brothers, dribbled around Jimmy and passed the ball to Sean Harmon, who dunked it.

"Turkey!" Sean looked down from his six-three frame and scoffed at Kevin.

Kevin looked over at Orion. His great-great-great-great-great-great-great-great-great-grandson's mouth was wide open. He was impressed.

"Anybody can do a simple dunk," Kevin said.

Kevin took the ball out and passed it in to Jimmy, who

missed the shot but got his own rebound. He passed the ball out to Kevin. Kevin shot, watched the ball roll off the ring and fall into the waiting hands of Sean Harmon.

"I got him! I got him!" Kevin yelled.

Sean dribbled toward the basket, took a huge step as he reached the lane, and went up, up, up. He twisted his body in the air and brought the ball down hard over his head in a vicious behind-the-back slam dunk!

"Lucky!" Kevin whispered. "You don't have any moves, man."

Sean took over the game. He dribbled around and over Kevin's team with a vengeance. He dunked with one hand, with two hands, on an alley-oop, and finally ended the game with a spinning three-sixty whammer-jammer dunk.

"See you guys later," Kevin said.

"Yeah, when you learn to play some ball," Eddie Farrell said.

"So, what do you think?" Kevin asked Orion as they reached his house.

"It was truly a wonderful experience," Orion said. "But did you decide if the goal was the goal of Good or Evil?"

"It was the goal of Good," Kevin said.

"And the flying magician reached it more than you," Orion said. "And still you are pleased."

"The goodness of the Goal is more important than those who seek it," Kevin said.

"How wise! How perfectly wise!" Orion said.

"Yeah, I guess so." Kevin nodded.

"I am . . . I am . . ." Orion was taking deep breaths.

"What's wrong?" Kevin asked.

"I am disintegrating again," Orion said. "Let me get

45

back into this small room. It's easier on my eyes in the darkness."

Kevin opened the door, and pushed aside some of his old sneakers so that Orion could sit inside the closet. When he closed the door he saw a faint glow around the edges.

"It has been a . . . wonderful . . . wonder . . . wonderful experience," came from the closet.

"Hey, I'm glad you came," Kevin said.

"It has been a . . . wonderful . . . experience," came yet another muffled call from the closet.

"Don't mention it," Kevin said.

The light from the closet grew brighter, and then suddenly disappeared. Kevin waited a long time. Finally, he went to the closet and opened it. The floor where Orion had been sitting was bare except for the sneakers and an old baseball with a torn cover.

The next day in school he ran into Jimmy on the way to the cafeteria.

"I don't know why you wanted to get us creamed like that," Jimmy said. "What did your friend have to think about it?"

"He thought it was a great game," Kevin said.

"What is he," Jimmy asked, "some kind of a wise guy?"

"No," Kevin answered with a broad smile. "I'm the wise guy."

About Walter Dean Myers

My earliest experience of being me was a reading experience. I remember being in Harlem and my mother working with me, teaching me to read. My foster parents weren't educated people. My mother often did day's work, that is, working by the day for people who needed their houses cleaned.

When she wasn't working my mother would sit with me in the afternoons and read romance magazines to me. I still remember sitting in that sunny room. Those moments with my mother were so pleasant, so deeply ingrained in my memory.

I lived in New York with my two sisters, my foster parents, and occasionally the father of my foster father. I didn't much like this old man. Especially I didn't like his scary stories. He told endless stories about the Garden of Eden, about Adam and Eve, and about the snake. Whatever I did he had an Old Testament story for the particular occasion.

I didn't like my grandfather because of his stories and sometimes I didn't like my father because of his stories, mostly spooky. But what my grandfather and father were doing, besides scaring me, was passing down their ideas of what life was about. There was the Old Testament, the idea of moral being and moral judgment. My grandfather had passed it down to my father and then to me. It seems I have continued the tradition and pass on my own stories.

Don't believe in ghosts? Take this dare. . . .

The Haunting of Fex O'Toole

CONSTANCE GREENE

T HE HOUSE looked out from narrow gloomy eyes. A cold wind snarled in and out of the row of beat-up pine trees that ringed the cobblestoned drive. From the top of the tallest pine an owl shrieked a warning.

Fex O'Toole came close to losing it then.

"Double dare you, Fexie," the voice behind him purred. "Go on in, see what's going on. Don't be scared. It's only a haunted house."

Gusts of laughter cold as any wind rose, snickers overcame the motley crew gathered there for fun and games. Fex wrapped his arms around himself for warmth, which did not come.

"Just climb those old stairs and go right on in," the voice continued. "You don't even have to knock."

Tell him to buzz off, said the little voice that lived inside Fex's head. *Tell them you're through with this nonsense.*

"A face! I saw a face upstairs! Looking out!" Barney Barnes, leader of the pack and longtime tormentor of Fex O'Toole, danced in a tight circle, clumsy as a circus bear, beside himself with excitement.

"Double dare you, Fex," Barney panted. "I swear to God I saw a face. Go on up, Fex. See who it is."

"I'm outa here," Fex said.

"You can do it. Double double dare," Barney said. "That's two doubles, in case you can't count." Barney raised his arms like a orchestra conductor and the rest laughed on cue.

"You go," Fex said. "It was your idea to come out here in the first place. I'm not getting sucked into this, Barney. You go. They won't hurt you. They'll only haunt you. Go on up yourself. I'm not doing your dirty work for you anymore."

Even to his own ears Fex's voice lacked conviction, sounded phony and a little hollow. Only last week his father had sat him down and given him a long, hard lecture on the dangers he was facing if he kept on doing stunts just because someone double-dared him to.

"For a smart kid, Fex," his father's voice rang now in his ears, "you're pretty dumb. These kids who egg you on are cowards. You won't catch them doing these things that they dare you to do. You're a patsy, Fex. Stand up to them. They have no guts and you do. And you're not a coward either. But you sure are playing the fool."

His father's eyes were angry and sorrowful. "Your mother and I are very sad about this double-dare business, Fex. We're afraid you'll get yourself in over your head someday if it continues."

Then, in a rare gesture, his father had laid a hand against Fex's cheek and Fex had to turn away to conceal the tears he felt crowding his eyes.

So here he was, playing the fool again, unable to stop himself.

"You can do it, Fex." Barney's voice was slow and soft, hypnotizing. Something surged in Fex's gut and threatened to spill out. He swallowed hard.

"I think it was a ghost I saw," Barney said. "It looked like one, all white and staring. I think I heard it moan too. You guys hear it moan?"

Barney's guys nodded their heads off.

"Ghosts don't hurt you. I heard if a person sees a ghost, their hair turns white overnight," Barney said. "That'd be cool, Fex. Just think, you'd be the only kid in the sixth grade with white hair. I wouldn't mind that." Barney smacked his lips noisily.

"You want white hair, be my guest," Fex said.

"There you go, Fexie. Attaboy. Go for it."

And although Barney hadn't laid a hand on him, Fex felt something urging him on. As if a large hand were in the middle of his back, pushing him, making him climb the rickety flight of steps, toward the murky windows, the enormous wooden door. With its brass handle.

Slowly, as if he were the master of his fate, the captain of his own soul, Fex put one foot after the other.

The gang let out its collective breath, sounding like a snake about to strike. A sinister, slippery, rasping sound, like a rattler on the prowl, Fex thought.

The house waited and watched. Fex kept his head down. If there was a face looking out of the upstairs window, he

didn't want to know about it. One, two, three, four steps.
Four more to go.

Back. Go back, Fex's little voice ordered.

But he plunged onward, ever onward.

"We'll wait here," Barney said, snickering. "If you need help, just holler."

Fex couldn't believe what he was doing. He took the last two steps in one bound and swaggered over to a window and looked in. Nothing. Then he pushed against the door, and to his utter astonishment it swung open slowly. His heart leapt in his throat and stuck there.

In the distance a dog barked. Ragged clouds bunched against the horizon, threatening rain. Soon it would be dark. Fex shivered and stepped into a long hall. Dust flew everywhere, churned by the outside air.

"There's nobody here," he called.

"Go upstairs!" Barney yelled. "It doesn't count until you go upstairs and see what's going on."

Like a robot Fex turned toward the stairs. Out of the corner of his eye he caught movement. Someone was there, watching. A person with a bone-white face and wide, staring eyes. Disheveled hair and a T-shirt that looked familiar. It was himself, Fex O'Toole, madman, prize jerk, all-time nerd. An eleven-year-old turkey, reflected in a long, cracked mirror on the opposite wall.

In an attempt at bravado he stuck out his tongue at himself and was pleased to see his reflection do the same. This room off the hall must once have been a living room, Fex decided as he wandered in. Mice droppings littered the floor. Spiderwebs as big as dinner plates swung from the ceiling. In the far corner something that looked like a mattress covered with a filthy sheet cowered. Last year some squatters had moved into this old and deserted and, some said, haunted house. They'd trashed the place and set a fire in one of the rooms, which brought out the volunteer fire department in record numbers. The rooms smelled of many things, among them dead ashes.

Three chairs leaned against one another for support, gathered together as if expecting visitors who would never come.

What am I doing here? Fex asked himself. He felt sad. This had once been someone's house. Home. Now it seemed a dwelling without life or hope.

His father's voice came again, loud and impatient.

"They're using you, Fex. Show them you're nobody's fool. This may lead to something you can't escape from. Get out while the getting's good, Fex."

Music rose, faint, faraway. He tipped his head, listening. Most likely it was from outside; Barney's boom box. Barney didn't go to the bathroom without that boom box. He claimed he'd ripped it off from K mart but Fex knew for a fact Barney's mother had given it to him for his birthday.

The music sounded tinny and unreal, like a flute or a violin gone sour. Fex was pretty sure it wasn't the TV or the radio. It sounded like someone practicing, someone without a shred of musical talent. Like his little brother Jerry. Jerry sawed away on his rented violin enthusiastically and every member of the O'Toole family fell on the floor laughing.

"Papa!"

The voice was so close, so unexpected, it almost blew Fex away. He leapt high in the air like a ballet dancer. It was a girl's voice, of that he was sure. He backed toward the door without taking his eyes away from the stairs. If it was a girl, he wanted to see her. He held his breath so no one would hear him go.

"Papa, there is someone here."

She had that right, all right.

Get out of here. Fex's heart thundered in his chest. *They're coming for you. Who is They?* Footsteps, light and quick, approached.

Suddenly, a terrible coldness filled the hall, a coldness unlike any he had ever felt. He tried to flee, to lift his feet, to call out for help, but it was as if he'd turned to stone.

"Cinda." A man's gruff voice rang out. "Cinda, your grandmother says your hair must be tended to. She says you must come to her room immediately and she will make you look presentable. Your bonnet must be tied properly and your shoes must be buttoned. You always miss a few buttons, she says, and it is important to have them right on this day, of all days."

A rustling sound filled the upstairs hall. "No, I won't!" Cinda cried, and Fex thought the grandmother was coming for her.

Or maybe for him.

"Cinda dear," the grandmother coaxed gently, "be a good child."

"Be quick now," said the man's gruff voice. "The coach will soon be here. We cannot keep it waiting. Button your shoes, Cinda. Please. Make haste."

"Papa, I hate to button my shoes. There are so many buttons. My fingers get all mixed up."

Try Velcro, Cinda. Velcro's easy. It beats buttons any

day. The words popped into Fex's head. Poor old Cinda didn't get the message. She went on and on about the buttons until the gruff voice cautioned.

"Your grandmother is losing her patience, child. As am I." Papa has had it, Fex thought.

Something rustled noisily, close by. Then faded into the distance. Fex backed tight up against the wall, making himself small, maybe even invisible. If They could be invisible, why couldn't he?

Then a thought shot into his head. They were pulling his leg. Not They with a capital *T,* but Barney and his band of bozos. It was all a put-up job. Maybe they were playing a tape of an old movie and Cinda was the star. Shirley Temple, maybe. If Cinda started to tap-dance, he'd know he was right.

Well, he'd show 'em. Fex O'Toole might be a pushover for a double dare, but he was no dummy.

"Hey, up there!" he shouted. "I'm not scared. You guys can come out now. I know you're there! Come on out!"

A terrible silence gripped the house. Fex felt a presence. He was not alone. Of that he was absolutely sure. A wave of whispers, harsh, sinister, scorched his ears. He listened very hard but couldn't make out any words. Just whispers, slipping, sliding around him.

They were trying to decide what to do with him.

Run for it. He heard his father's voice. Go.

No, stay, the voice in Fex's head said. *There is more to come. Stay. You may never get another chance.*

Chance at what?

"Cinda, I hear the horses. It is time. Come along."

54

Heavy footsteps paced back and forth overhead. "The coach is here at last."

If Barney is out there, he'll freak, Fex thought. *A coach and horses with one of those characters wearing a red coat and a top hat sitting up top. Barney will just freak out.*

In his mind's eye he imagined Barney and his brood clotted in a nervous little group, checking the purple sky for thunderclouds. Then along came the coach and horses. Oh, but that would blow their tiny little minds!

He wanted Barney to go, wanted him to stay. He was at the brink of a precipice, about to learn some rare and long-hidden truth. Goose bumps crawled up Fex's arms and settled behind his ears and along his neck in a neat row.

"Stop! You're hurting me!" the girl's voice wailed. "You're pulling my hair. Why do you pull and tug so? It hurts."

A voice murmured something.

"Help me, Papa. The buttons are too big for my hands."

Fex reached out. He would help her do up her shoes. She must not miss the coach at the door. If the shoes weren't buttoned, she might trip and fall. As he did when he raced downstairs to catch the school bus and fell over his untied laces. That would never do.

"Clumsy oaf!" Was that his brother Pete shouting, or was it Papa?

"There now, Cinda. Ready at last," Papa said.

"You look lovely, child."

A rush of cold air came first. Then they were at the door. In a small, violent commotion they were gone. Fex thought he heard the unmistakable sharp sound of horses' hooves on the cobblestones. A wave of cold followed down the stairs behind them. Cold was their constant companion.

He was alone. The house rang with emptiness. He had never been so alone.

Fex went to a window. Now that They were gone, his feet did his bidding. He looked out, hoping to see the coach and horses racing into the distance. Surely that would prove something, if he saw horses.

Nothing was there. Nothing. There was no trace of Barney, or any of his little men. Even the wind had gone. The trees were motionless.

A crackling sound came from overhead. Fex looked up and a piece of plaster fell from the ceiling, striking him full in the face. As it hit him, the plaster made a small popping sound, like a gun.

I'm hit, Fex thought as he fell. *They killed me. It is Their revenge. Because I came here and it was none of my business to come here. I disturbed Them. It is Their house. I broke the rules. So now, maybe I'm dead.*

But his eyes were still open. Plaster dust filled them, as well as his nose and mouth and ears. He staggered to his feet, blinded by the dust, which swirled thickly around him.

Putting his arms straight out in front of himself, he felt his way toward where he thought the door should be. At last he bumped his head against the wall and felt for the doorknob.

There it was. He laid hold and pulled and tugged. Miraculously, the door opened and night air rushed in.

Outside, it was absolutely still. The landscape was motionless, calm. The bunched clouds had disappeared from the horizon and the sky was lighter than it had been. The east was filled with a yellow light and Fex, amazed, thought, *I've been out all night. It's almost dawn. It isn't night, it's morning.*

He began to run. His mother and father would be beside themselves. His father would be very angry, his mother frantic with worry. They'd think something terrible had happened to him.

At the end of the driveway he paused to look back at the house. It stared at him with narrow gloomy eyes. There were no lights, no faces, at any window. It was just a lonely, decrepit old house.

He had imagined the whole thing.

He ran the rest of the way home. When he rounded the corner of his street, he could see lights blossoming in every window of his house. He forced himself to run the rest of the way, his heart threatening to burst from his chest. What damage there was had been done. Why hurry now? Still he ran.

Panting like a dog that's been out chasing rabbits, he almost fell into the kitchen, catching his mother with her feet propped on the kitchen table, reading the paper.

"My heavens, Fex, where on earth have you been?"

Her feet came off the table fast, with a sharp smacking sound. She told *him* not to put *his* feet on the table and there *she* was. If he'd had the energy, he would've given her a hard time.

"Well, look who's here," Pete sneered. "Lucky for you Dad's working late tonight, else you'd probably be grounded for about a hundred years. Mom was worried about you. How come you didn't call?"

Pete stuck his face into Fex's face.

"Get your face out of here or I'll punch you into the middle of next week," Fex said.

Startled, Pete pulled back.

"You look like you just saw a ghost," Pete said.

"I did," said Fex.

Jerry wrinkled his nose and said, "You smell."

"It's only plaster dust," Fex said.

"I've told you not to play around construction sites," his mother said. "They can be dangerous."

"Stinks is more like it," Pete said.

His mother sniffed. "Horse manure is what it smells like. Where did you find any horses around here, Fex? As far as I know, there are none for miles."

Fex examined his feet. Turned up his sneakers, right, then left, to check out the soles. Sure enough, both soles were loaded with horse manure. Stuffed tightly into every crack and cranny.

"Better take those off, Fex, hop into a shower," his mother said. "I'll see if I can get that stuff out with a scrub brush."

"Your face is all white," Pete said. "So's your hair. You look like a clown, you clown."

"Hey, Fex." Jerry's thin little face broke into a broad grin. "I got a neat idea. Don't wash your hair and when you go to school tomorrow, you'll be the only kid in the sixth grade who has white hair. That'd be cool."

"Good idea, Jerry," Fex said.

"Show-off," Pete said.

About Constance Greene

I believe in ghosts. I have never seen one but that doesn't stop me from thinking that ghosts may really exist. I like to think that the spirit of people I've loved might return someday, as I've heard and read they do.

"The Haunting of Fex O'Toole" is my first ghost story. Fex is the hero of my book *Double-Dare O'Toole.* And, as the title suggests, Fex has a problem. He is unable to resist a double dare. As a result he gets into all kinds of trouble: humiliating, embarrassing, sometimes even life threatening.

And no matter how angry his parents get, no matter how often his father lectures him about what a fool he is to accept these double dares, Fex seems unable to break this bad habit.

The scene of this story is an empty house: run-down, deserted, spooky. A proper haunted house. Barney Barnes, local bad guy, double-dares Fex to go inside this house and check it for ghosts. Fex resists, but in the end he slowly walks up the rickety steps and pushes open the big old door and walks in.

What he finds there is exciting, scary, and, to my mind, perfectly possible. I wish it had happened to me.

Constance Greene's most recent novels are *Odds on Oliver* and *Nora: Maybe a Ghost Story.*

A wager with the devil . . .

Variation on a Theme: The Grateful Dead

JUDITH GOROG

*A*T TWILIGHT on a dusty path far from here, a woman pulls her cloak more closely around her, muttering about the coming darkness. Seeing a motionless form on the ground just off the way, she makes a wide circle to avoid it, staring at it the whole time. She is afraid, hurrying to reach her house in the village before dark. As the woman scurries past, she thinks that the clothes it wears are strange; certainly they don't belong to anybody she knows. It might be a wandering beggar, or a robber just waiting to pounce once her back is turned.

Bending forward, the woman walks faster, never slackening her pace until at last she is close to the lights of the village. It is quite dark by the time a burly man draws near the still form by the side of the path. He walks over to it, nudges it with his foot, saying, "What's this? If not dead, then close enough, I say. And not needing those fine boots for tomorrow." He kneels down, takes off the boots, and seeing the socks are of soft warm stuff and not a bit worn, the thief takes them as well before he continues on his way.

The next to pass is a man on horseback, thinking of the food and warm fire that will be there for him in the tavern in that village not so far away. With his eyes on the road ahead he doesn't really notice the dark lump on the ground.

The moon is up by the time a fourth traveler comes along the path. Seeing the barefoot body, he stops. With one swift motion he removes a warm cloak from it, saying, "I need this away far more than you do," and wraps it around himself as he continues on the path.

A few hours before dawn, after the moon has set and the night grown bitter cold, a young man approaches the place where the body lies beside the path. He has walked all night, hoping to reach his mother's kitchen in time for breakfast, a meal he yearns to taste. He was ten years old when the army snatched him out of his parents' courtyard, took him to be a drummer boy. Now, seven years later, he is discharged, hoping never to serve again, though you never can tell about the army.

Seeing the body, he stops, kneels down. It is a woman, not young, but with thick silver hair, fine soft skin, dressed in foreign clothes that are not shabby in the least.

The drummer takes off his pack. There, at the bottom, under his sticks and the clean linen, is the shovel all soldiers must carry. Taking the shovel, he looks for a place where he can dig. It is not easy, with roots, rocks, and the cold night earth, but the drummer starts to dig a proper grave, thinking meanwhile of how the soldiers had talked of death, of how others had feared to lie unburied, how they had made promises to one another.

When the digging is especially hard, he wonders if he has made the right decision. After all, he has seen and heard of places where the dead were not buried. The drummer continues digging, for he knows of no place where the dead are dumped by the side of the road.

When at last the hole is deep enough, the drummer carries the body to the place.

"Ma'am, I don't know what you'd want said or done, but I'll give you what my old comrades would have wanted, and I know my mother would want to face the rising sun, so here it is."

With that he places the body into the grave, covers her face with his last clean handkerchief, says those words he'd said at other times, and fills in the grave. On top of the earth he places the stones he'd uncovered in the digging, adding a few more to make it look right. He cleans his hands as best he can on the long meadow grass near the spot, takes out his sticks, and softly drums the pattern used by his regiment for the burying of the dead.

The whole time, the drummer boy is somewhat afraid, thinking that if anyone sees him, he could well be hanged as a murderer. At last, as the pink light of morning fills the sky, the drummer, now sweating, muddy, and certain not to arrive in time for breakfast, continues on his way.

His first night home, the drummer sleeps the sleep of

the dead. The second night he dances until the break of day. On the third night, just after midnight, he is deep asleep in the bed he shares with his four brothers, when he is abruptly awakened by someone calling him, "Drummer! Drummer! Wake up! I have been waiting for you. We must hurry!"

The drummer sits up in bed, while his brothers sleep peacefully on. He sees, standing at the foot of the bed, the woman he had buried on the way home, and he is afraid.

"Come," the woman says.

"No," replies the drummer, thinking she is a vampire or some other creature of the regions of the dead. "I did no harm to you. You have no claim on me."

"Please," says the woman. The accents in which she speaks are so foreign to the drummer that he must strain to understand her speech.

"Please," she urges. "There is very little of time as you, the living, perceive it, given to this ghostly form of mine. I thank you. Come with me, and everything will be explained to you, and no harm will come to you. I ask you to trust me. Please."

During his years away from home the drummer has acquired a bit of a taste for danger, so he gets out of bed and goes with the ghost of the foreign woman.

It is not an easy journey. The ghost of the foreign woman places her cold hand on his, and they set off at a run. The drummer needs all his strength to travel as they do, through the regions of the dead, his ears filled with the cries of the lonely. At last they stand before the massive door of a great house in a strange city.

"Knock," whispers the ghost of the foreign woman. Her

colors are fading so that now she is nearly transparent. Her strength, too, seems to be fading. When the door opens, she staggers inside. The drummer remains there at the entrance, not certain what to do next.

A tall bearded man motions for him to enter, then leads him to a room in which a fire burns, a room hung with silks, a room in which there are shelves of scrolls, books, musical instruments, three chairs before the fire. Lamps throw a pleasing glow upon a table laden with food and drink.

"Your Grace." The bearded man addresses the ghost of the foreign woman in a voice tender with affection.

"You must tell him," the ghost of the foreign woman replies. "I am on my way." Her face is momentarily bright with a smile of relief and joy.

"Thank you. Thank you" are the last words they hear, as, with a rush of air that makes the fire dance, she is gone.

"Please," says the bearded man after a few moments. "Sit down. You and I can still eat and drink. And I can tell you what has happened.

"Her Grace is, *was,* of the blood royal. I, who have served her these many years, am of the greater nobility of this, our country."

He hands the drummer a cup, touches the rim of his own to it, and drinks.

"You see." he leans back, studies the face of the drummer for a time, then continues. "Her Grace did live a long, long life, and it was, at some times, a life of excess."

The drummer, polite, but not quite understanding, repeats, "Excess?"

"She did some wicked things, and felt, as death approached, that perhaps the one you would call the devil had a fair grip upon her soul. To save herself from the devil she made a wager with him."

The drummer's eyes widen.

"Her Grace bet the devil that he could place her dead body anywhere on earth; that is to say where there are some inhabitants. Her Grace said to the devil, 'I wager my soul upon it that I can count on the kindness of a stranger to give me burial before dawn.' "

"You came upon her after she had been twice robbed, twice more simply passed by."

The drummer blushes, looks down at the cup in his hands.

"The devil has already been here tonight," says the bearded man. "I was expecting you."

"Was he angry that she beat him?" asks the drummer.

The bearded man puts the tips of his fingers together in front of his face, stares a moment at the fire, before he replies.

"Your reward for your kindness to a stranger is that you are now rich, heir to most of the vast fortune of her late Grace. The devil arrived here tonight rubbing his hands with a show of glee, saying that he feels he has actually made quite a good wager with her Grace. You see, the devil admitted that he has lost one soul, hers, but claimed that now he has a very good chance indeed at the souls of the two thieves who robbed her, and at those who ignored her, and . . ."

"And?" asks the drummer, feeling a chill.

"And the devil claimed to be patient beyond all measure. He was sitting right where you are now, smiling and smiling, when he remarked, 'Who knows what great wealth will do to the soul of that young drummer?'"

About Judith Gorog

Judith Gorog is a writer of odd stories who lives in Lancaster, Pennsylvania, with her family. Two of her children listen to the Grateful Dead, so that Gorog over the years has heard many hours of Dead tapes and has read about the Dead and their shows. Early in 1992 Gorog attended the New York Public Library celebration of Books for the Teen Age, where Mickey Hart's *Drumming at the Edge of Magic* was one of the books honored as a favorite of teenage readers—the second time the book had been strongly recommended.

The story printed here came out of the music and the reading. It is a variation on an old tale, in which a person kind enough to bury a dead person is then rewarded with riches by the grateful dead.

Other Gorog stories may be found in her collections and novels: *A Taste For Quiet; Caught in the Turtle; No Swimming in Dark Pond; Three Dreams and a Nightmare; In a Messy, Messy Room; Winning Scheherazade; On Meeting Witches at Wells; Tiger Lily; Zilla Sasparilla and the Mud Baby; Beware! A Collection of Terrifying, Occasionally Funny Baby-sitter Stories,* and coming next year, *In the Gallery Pitu,* a collection of stories connected with a very strange artist, and a gallery you may enter using virtual reality with your TV set, or, if you have the courage, visit in person.

The Face in the Rafters

JANET TAYLOR LISLE

"THIS IS a real ghost story. It isn't for children," my father always began.

That was the signal. We'd move in close to him.

"There's no blood and guts in it, no clanking chains or ruby-eyed vampires," he'd go on. "There aren't any green hands crawling by themselves into someone's bedroom at night, and no one hears a heart beating under the floor-boards. All that stuff is for kids. This story's the real thing. Because it happened."

"Please, John. Not that story," my mother usually broke in, about then. "I really would prefer another. Any other."

My father would smile grimly at this.

"Your mother is right. We would both prefer another story," he'd say. "We would like to be rid of this wretched tale, to never think of it or have to dream of it again.

68

Unfortunately, it has chosen us. There's no escape. What can we do but go on telling it, if only in self-defense?"

By this time all of us children would be practically on top of my father, who was sometimes on the beach sitting around a campfire, sometimes in a cabin with a woodstove crackling nearby. There were five children in our family, four boys and a girl. I was both the oldest and the girl, which put me in the superior position of being sharper and having the longest memory.

I remember my father told the story after Thanksgiving dinner one time and my Aunt Adele fainted. Another night we were on a cruising boat moored off the coast of Maine, and the wind was howling outside, and the mast was creaking, and my mother begged him to stop, but he refused.

"This is a story that cannot be stopped," my father said, looking each of us, by turn, in the eye. "It's a story that has joined up with real life, woven itself into our lives, your mother's and mine, until we can't tell which is which, story or life. We can't tell where one ends and the other begins."

"Oh, John, really!" my mother would exclaim. She had a theory that kids can't tell the difference between what is real and what is made up, and might get permanently damaged by hearing the wrong thing. "You're scaring these poor children to death. How do you expect them to settle down and go to sleep after—"

"Sleep!" my father would roar, while my brothers glanced nervously at me and I grinned back. "This is no time for sleep. How could anyone sleep knowing there is a chance that you and I"—he grasped my mother's hand and lowered his voice to a stage whisper—"may not even live to see how the story ends!"

"John!" The hand was snatched away. "You go too far. I will not stand for—"

"Come on! Come on! Tell it!" I'd start yelling to drown her out. Dad's story had a fascination for me I can't explain. Then all my little brothers would chime in. They always watched me to see how to act. Some people think that boys are naturally brave, that they're born that way and will be that way no matter what. But that isn't true. A lot of boys are jittery in the beginning. They get brave by watching how strong people around them act, especially strong people like their older sisters.

Sometimes, just as my father began to tell the story, one of my brothers would crawl into my lap.

"This story isn't really true, is it?" he'd whisper, to make sure.

"Don't worry," I always answered. "It's only a ghost story."

Your mother and I were very much in love when we married. For our honeymoon we decided to go away by ourselves to someplace off the beaten track where we could be thoroughly alone.

[My father always started the ghost story this way, at which point, inevitably, one or another of my little brothers would pipe up and want to know what, exactly, a honeymoon was, or whether he should go to the bathroom now or later. Then my father would close his mouth and stare at the ceiling while the culprit was hustled out of the room, or nudged to one side for an explanation. Only when the interruption was taken care of, and we were all sitting silent around him again, did he lower his eyes and continue. A good ghost story requires silence, he said once, out of respect for the unseen powers in our world.]

Our plan was to drive straight north to the mountains until we came upon a place lonely and quiet enough to please us, and then to look for lodgings [my father went on]. We brought our sleeping bags with us in the car, and several boxes of food, and a propane stove and lantern in case there was no electricity. We were sensible travelers who knew how to plan ahead. There wasn't much we didn't feel we could handle.

All one day we drove, first by highway, and then on two-lane state roads, and finally, as we got deeper into the mountains, on narrow, twisting back roads where we met few cars and the trees stooped low over our heads. At the first sign of dark we began looking for a place to stop. There wasn't a lot to choose from.

"What about that?" your mother said at last, pointing to a group of cabins set away from the road. They were newly painted, white with green shutters. Each house had a window box out front filled with summer flowers. The place looked comfortable and ordinary and we drove right in.

The rental office was in the front cabin. The man behind the counter was a leathery old soul, but he had a quick eye.

"So, up here on your honeymoon, are you?" he barked, almost as soon as we came in the door.

That embarrassed us. One of the reasons we had traveled so far out into the country was to escape this very sort of notice.

"Of course not," I protested. "We've been married for

71

years. We're just up here on a trip, getting away for some rest. Have you got a cabin we could rent for four or five days?"

The old fellow didn't look much convinced by my reply. He bent over a rumpled registration book and tapped a dried-up finger on the page.

"I'm full," he said. "Every night this week."

"Full!" your mother exclaimed. "But there's not one car parked out front."

The old man's eye veered over to her and looked her up and down.

"I'm full, I tell you," he said. "The cabins are booked. Traveling salesmen for the most part. They'll get in late tonight. Anyways, you two don't want to stay here, being who and what y'are." He gave your mother another piercing stare.

I stepped forward.

"Whoever and whatever you think we are has nothing to do with this," I told him fiercely. (I was aware that your mother was watching me, and I wanted to make a good impression.) "We need a place to stay for the night, for several nights, in fact, if the price is reasonable. We've come a long way and are tired. Surely you can fit us in somewhere here?"

The desk clerk sighed when he heard this. It was almost as if he'd seen it happen before and knew the uselessness of trying to make a change.

"So it's to be that way, is it?" he muttered, more to himself than us.

"It is," I announced grandly.

"There's Brower's shack, then. Not much of a place, one

room and no electricity. No plumbing either; you'll have to make use of the great outdoors. There's bunks, though, and a big fireplace. You're welcome to a load of wood I've got stacked out back here. Can't say you'll be very comfortable, but . . . Are you sure you aren't honeymooners?" he said, peering at us again. "I don't often make a mistake about that."

"We'll take the shack," your mother declared. She's always been a person to think for herself.

The truth was, Brower's sounded wonderful to both of us. It sounded like the very place we'd had in mind when we'd planned our trip. And when the old desk clerk had shown us where the woodpile was, and directed us down an overgrown path in back of the other cabins, we arrived to find that Brower's was just as we'd hoped: simple, quiet, away from the world.

It was an old wooden cabin, probably once a hunter's retreat. Inside, the floor was a bit dusty, but there was a table, some thick candles, and a couple of chairs. We brought in our food and our sleeping bags, and set ourselves up in no time. That night we heated a big can of Dinty Moore beef stew on our propane stove, and toasted hunks of bread over the fire, and were as happy as any new-married couple ever were. We dragged the mattresses off the bunk beds into the middle of the floor, where we could put them together. Then we bundled under the sleeping bags and snuffed the candles, and after a while we fell sound asleep.

It must have been past midnight when I woke and found myself on my back, looking into darkness. What roused me, I can't say for sure, but it seemed that I heard the cheerful whistling of some passerby outside, though it may have been a bird chirping in the forest.

In any case, I was gazing upward sleepily, when suddenly I jolted wide awake. A face was watching me from the rafters over my head. It was very pale, thin-lipped, with eyes that shone faintly in the light cast by our dying fire. There was no sign of the rest of a body. I suppose it was hidden in the rafters' shadows, though how it balanced there, I couldn't guess. Ghostly and disconnected, the face floated above me, and I knew it was real because its mouth began to grin. Then the lips moved and a coarse half-whisper reached my ears.

"Your human destiny has been foretold! Prepare! Prepare! The hour of your death is known. Darkness waits on every road to your future!"

The eyes looked at me without blinking and there followed a terrible pause, as if I were expected to make some reply. But my mouth had locked shut and I could only stare back in horror. At length the specter spoke again, informing me of the exact date—the day, the month, and the year—upon which my life on earth would end. Then its lips broke into an even more hideous leer, and the whole dreadful thing vanished from sight.

Well, by now, as you can imagine, my heart was pounding and I was cold with fright. I wanted to wake your mother at once to tell her what had happened. But when I looked at her, she was sleeping so peacefully, without a care in the world, that I thought I couldn't disturb her. So I lay on alone with my wild vision, trying to think what it could mean, and after a long while I slept again.

Next morning the sun was streaming through the windows when we awoke, and a great chorus of birds sang outside, reminding us of how far into the wilderness we'd come. Anyone would think that we should have been the two happiest people in the world, but a gloom had settled over us. Your mother did not look well. At first she pretended that nothing was wrong, and tried to carry on with some trivial conversation. But soon, she confided to me that she had dreamed a most terrible dream during the night, and could not seem to shake it off.

"A dream?" I asked sharply. "What was it about?"

"There was someone whistling in the distance, a strange tune I'd never heard," your mother said. "Then I seemed to look up in the rafters. A horrible white face was there, looking down at me."

"That was no dream! I saw it too," I cried out. "Did it speak?"

"It did," your mother answered, her voice dropping to a whisper. "It predicted the day of my death."

We clasped hands, then, and looked up together at the rafters above the mattresses. There was nothing there now. We walked back and forth examining every part of the cabin's roof. We went outside to check for footprints, or signs of forced entry. There were none. Finally, we sat on the cabin's front stoop and considered what to do. Nothing like this had ever happened to either of us. We were sensible people who did not believe in ghosts. If a face had appeared in the rafters, it must have some explanation. Should we notify the desk clerk? Should we call the police?

"Do you think it's possible that similar dreams arose in our brains last night?" your mother said. "I've occasionally heard of such things happening."

"What date did the face predict for your end?" I asked her in return.

"I'll tell you, but you must also tell me yours," your mother said. "And on one condition. That we both swear never to reveal our dates to another person. Never. No matter what becomes of us. Whether we are really doomed or not, this is information that must remain secret, or it could be used against us."

I agreed immediately. But when I bent close and whispered my fateful hour, she jumped away and covered her ear.

"It is the same hour and day as mine!" your mother cried out.

From that moment we were both thoroughly spooked, for though the dreams of two sleepers may sometimes resemble each other, their details will never, in the natural course of events, be identical. We were packed within a half hour. We decided not to mention the event to anyone. It made such a ridiculous story: a whistle, a face, a doomsday prediction. We wanted, simply, to get away. But as we paid our bill at the front desk, the suspicious old clerk inquired how our night at Brower's had gone.

"Oh, fine!" I replied heartily, trying to draw him off the track. "We've decided to head home early, that's all. It's a great old place."

"That so?" The fellow cocked his head skeptically. "There's strange rumors about that cabin. Most people from these parts won't go near it since the young couple was found there."

"What young couple?" your mother dared to ask.

"I suppose I may as well tell you, since you've had such a

plain and ordinary night," the desk clerk replied, his eyes sliding over us. "Twenty-five years ago a young couple on their honeymoon was found hung in that cabin, lynched from the rafters, side by side. It was murder, clear as could be, and the police soon found the killer. He was a local man who'd wanted the bride for himself, and predicted the lovers' end if they ever swore vows in a church. Notes were found in his possession setting the time and place of their deaths. He was convicted and sent away to prison for life, where he eventually hung himself from the bars of his own cell. But . . ." The desk clerk paused.

"But what?" your mother and I asked in a single breath.

"Well, the incident caused quite a stir around here, and perhaps because of that, imaginations started to run wild. It's said other couples who've had the misfortune to honeymoon in that cabin have come to bad ends. One pair was crushed in a car crash just last year. Another couple was shot on a hunting expedition, not far from here. There've been others. One way or another they end up dying together. It's probably coincidence, but some folks wonder if somehow the killer is back, watching over that cabin and—"

"Don't tell us," I said quickly. Your mother's face had turned so pale. "We must be on our way."

"Oh, you needn't worry," the desk clerk called after us. "It's only honeymooners that come in for trouble. The cabin doesn't bother anyone else. Whistling Jack, that's what the fellow was called around here. I knew him. He seemed like a happy boy, always whistling a tune, going about his work with a smile on his face."

My father always stopped the story here. He'd wink at

my mother and look around at us to see how we were faring. Then, usually, one of my little brothers would speak up in a quivery voice.

"What's the date?" he'd ask.

"What?" My father pretended to look confused. "What date do you mean?"

"You know! The date foretold for your deaths. When is it? We're your children. We should know."

"Oh, that," my father said. "Well, I'm sorry, but I can't tell you. If you remember, I swore an oath to your mother and she swore one to me. We're afraid of what might happen if we broke our word."

"So the day hasn't passed?" another brother would ask. "Whistling Jack's prediction might still come true?"

"I'm afraid so," my father would say apologetically. "As long as I'm sitting here telling this ghost story, I guess you could say the tale's not ended yet."

"As long as you're sitting here telling this ghost story," my mother would break in irritably, at this point, "you might remind these poor, shaking children that none of this ever happened. You made it all up. We went to Bermuda for our honeymoon, not the mountains. We never spent the night in a haunted cabin and we never saw that silly face in the rafters."

"Is that true, Dad?" all my little brothers would yell, jumping up. Right then is when I'd see my mother catch his eye. It was the smallest flick of a glance but it told me everything.

"Of course it's true," I'd announce, as loud as I could, while my father gazed at me sharply. Then he'd proceed to gather everyone around him again, and sit us down. He'd look us each, by turn, in the eye.

"Your mother is right," he'd say, with complete seriousness. "I don't know what came over me, scaring you with a story like that. I guess the only way to make up for it is to tell you a real ghost story. Now, this next one is the honest-to-goodness truth, and I'm not kidding. There aren't any werewolves in it, and nobody drinks anyone else's blood, but it's the real real thing. I know," he'd say, looking straight at my mother, "because it happened. . . ."

About Janet Taylor Lisle

I grew up in Farmington, Connecticut, the eldest of five children and the only girl. "The Face in the Rafters" is a title I borrowed from a story that my father told many times around campfires and in dim-lit cabins when we were young. He called it a ghost story, but that did not stop us from looking under its surface and seeing real shadows.

Was it true that my mother disliked the story? We could never be sure. Did my father tell the story to tease her, or to prepare us all for a tragedy? We couldn't tell. There was something odd about the way he returned to the story again and again, as if, as he said, he could not escape it. Even when we children knew every line of his story by heart, and all the rhythms and risings and fallings of his voice, we still did not know if it was truth or make-believe, fact or the real ghost story my father protested it was. What is a "real ghost story" anyway? Readers of "The Face in the Rafters" may feel inspired to look into the question.

Those who take an interest in this tale may want to ask what has become of my parents, whether they really did meet their fate together, as the story predicted they would. Here, unfortunately, I must pull the thick curtain allotted to every writer of fiction, and plead my need for privacy in real life. If I wanted to write about myself and my family in that way, I would have become a biographer. No, no! I am a shy author, a private person, fit only for writing stories about the stories of my life.

Janet Taylor Lisle, who has long been interested in reality's borderlands, has published five books for children, including *Afternoon of the Elves,* a 1989 Newbery Honor Book, and *The Great Dimpole Oak,* which received the 1987 Golden Kite Honor Award. Her most recent book, *The Lampfish of Twill,* was a School Library Journal Best Book of 1990.

Here
and
Now

"I'll never leave you. . . ."

The Sounds of the House

GARY SOTO

T HREE DAYS after her mother was buried, the house
began to creak and moan, even without the shudder
of wind or her father's late-night footsteps to the bathroom. In her bed, which she shared with her six-year-old
sister, Angela, Maria could make out these sounds, thinking they were telling her something—creak from their
small living room, moan in the faraway bathroom. *Is that
Mama?* she thought. *What is she asking?* Maria listened
with the covers to her throat. She listened and then
stopped listening when a horn of moon glared through her
window, splashing the bed with moonlight the color of
spoons. She propped herself up on an elbow and watched
the moon tugging along a few stars. *The moon is far away,*
she lamented, *and so is Mother.*

She fell asleep only after the moon moved west and her
bedroom darkened. The next morning Maria rose from bed

without disturbing Angela, who lay on her hip gnashing her teeth in sleep. Her father was at the kitchen table, his face gray in the early morning light. He was drinking coffee, a pile of papers in front of him.

"Buenos días," Maria said, almost in a whisper.

When he raised his head and saw Maria, he opened his arms and beckoned her. She approached her father slowly and let her body into his arms. She could smell his cologne and the work of cement in his clothes. She could smell his sadness.

She pushed away and ironed down his hair with the flat of her hand. "Papi, you look sleepy," she said softly. "You need a shave."

"Tired, not sleepy, *mi'ja.*" He rubbed his chin and remarked with a lightness in his voice, "I might grow me a *bigote.*"

"Do you want something to eat?" Maria asked as she gazed over her shoulder at the refrigerator. Maria was thirteen, a good cook for a seventh grader, and felt that she should now be more responsible.

He ran a hand across his face and, lips pursed, wagged his head. But he raised his coffee cup, which Maria took. While she stood at the stove and reheated the coffee, she looked up at her mother's coffee mug that hung on a hook under the cupboard. Maria thought of taking it down now, but instead she took another cup, her own, and poured herself coffee, a habit that had not been allowed by her mother.

"Are you going to work today?" Maria asked as she handed her father his coffee. He had stayed home for a week and was now restless to get out of the house. It was

84

late spring, and the lawns were deep green and scraggly from months of hard winter rains.

He blew on the coffee, blew three times, and sipped from the edge cautiously.

"Sí," he answered. "It's better that I work, that I forget." He looked up with the twilight of sadness in his eyes and sighed. "Your mother was a good person—"

"I know," Maria said, cutting him off gently before he got started on the story of their lives.

Feeling sorry for him, for herself, she sat down next to her father and looked at the papers in front of him. They were filled with doodling for a paving job.

"Your math is wrong, Papi," she said after she had inspected his figures. "Mira."

"¿Qué?"

"It should be three hundred, not two hundred. You forgot the one."

She pointed a finger at his math, and her father, squinting over the pages, said in a laughing voice, "I've been cheating myself all my life, mi'ja. That's why we can't get ahead."

Maria was fixing the math for him when she heard a creak. She cocked an ear and listened. The creak sounded again, this time louder. She let out a squeak and let the pencil jump from her fingers when she heard yet another creak and the scraping of a chair.

"¿Qué pasó?" Father asked.

"Did you hear that?"

Her father raised his head and looked around. "No," he said after a moment of thought, "No oí nada."

The door just then swung open to reveal Angela, the

little sister, who stood sleepily with a stuffed whale pinched under her arm. She asked, "What's for breakfast?," lower lip pouting.

Since their mother's death, Angela had been acting spoiled and would throw a tantrum at the least provocation. And in the past week she had gotten all kinds of toys, including Rollerblades and a three-ring swimming pool that they blew up with an air pump. When she became bossy, their father let her have her way. He was sad and troubled by the accident that had taken his wife, their mother, an accident that shouldn't have happened. Their car's front left tire, a retread, had blown on a country road and the car careened not toward a bush or harmlessly into an empty field but toward an orange tree anchored into the valley earth.

"Do you want an *huevo*?" Maria asked.

"No, I want some hot chocolate," Angela said. "I'm cold."

As Angela crawled into her father's lap, thumb in her mouth, Maria went to the refrigerator and brought out a carton of milk. She splashed a cupful of milk into a saucepan and then heaped three spoonfuls of chocolate into a cup.

Angela looked over at Maria, who was watching the milk come to a hissing boil. "I want to use Mommy's cup," she snapped.

"It's Mama's cup, Angela."

"I want to use her cup!"

"Stop it! Quit acting like that!"

"Mommy's dead! She don't care!"

"*Cállate,*" their father cried angrily, turning Angela

toward him and shaking his daughter, so that the stuffed whale fell from her arms. Angela began to cry and wiggle from his arms. She collapsed to the floor, a bundle of grief.

Their father sighed and picked up his daughter, cooing his *sorry*s into her hair.

"Okay, you baby," Maria said, a frown on her face, and took the cup from the hook. When she turned over the cup, she discovered a smear of lipstick on the rim. She crossed herself and muttered, *"Ay, Dios,"* under her breath, a zipper of fear riding up her back.

Maria fixed her little sister her chocolate and then started to leave the kitchen in a hurry.

"¿Qué pasa, Maria?" Father called. "What's wrong?"

"Nothing," she answered. She ran to her bedroom and closed the door. She sat on her bed, knees to her chest and cuddling herself, trying to warm her body that had grown cold with fear as she remembered her mother's words— *"Mi'ja,* I will never leave you. I will always be with you." She rolled over onto her stomach, buried her face in her soft blankets, and started crying. But she stopped crying when she heard a crinkling sound, like the sound of paper being crushed into a ball. *Is it Mother?* she wondered. *Has she come back?* She turned and looked through her tears, scooting into the corner of the bed in fear. It was her kitten walking on her homework on the desk. She wiped her eyes and muttered, "You stupid thing. You scared me!" She flung a sock at the cat, who meowed and jumped from the desk, begging for attention. The cat leapt onto the bed and Maria took the cat into her arms.

"Are you sad?" Maria asked the cat. "We never got to say good-bye to Mommy."

"Maria, *ven acá*," Maria heard her father call from the living room. She could hear his heavy work boots ringing on the floor. She pushed the cat aside and jumped off her bed. Angela came into the bedroom. She was sipping from their mother's coffee cup, a mustache of chocolate staining her upper lip.

"I want some more," Angela said, holding up the cup like a chalice.

Ignoring her sister, Maria slipped on a sweatshirt, combed her hair in big long rips, and stomped out of the room with Angela trailing behind, begging for more chocolate.

"I want some more," Angela whined.

"All right!" Maria scolded as she stopped and wheeled around, hair whipping her shoulders. She hesitated at first in taking the cup from Angela but finally reached for it. She weighed it in her palm like an orange, thinking that it would weigh no more than a feather. But it was heavy as stone.

"*Me voy,* I'm off," Father told them. His face was shaved and his hair slicked back. "I want you two to stay home today. Tomorrow you can go to school." He gave them each a hug, squeezing love from their small bodies and whispering that they should be good. He gave them each a stick of chewing gum and trudged to the front door, swinging his heavy black lunch pail. The screen door slammed and he was gone.

Maria looked down at the cup in her hand, then her sister, who was scratching a mosquito bite on her thigh.

"What's wrong?" Maria asked.

"It hurts."

"Put some spit on it."

Leaving her to scratch her bites, Maria went off to the kitchen to fix her sister another cup of hot chocolate. *I should be good to her,* she figured. *It'll make Papi happy.*

As she was pouring the steaming milk into the cup, Maria noticed a new smear of red lipstick on the cup. "It's Mom's," she whispered to herself, and gazed around the kitchen, her eyes falling on the table where her mother would sit in solitude admiring her backyard and its flush of flowers. "Mom," she called in the direction of the table. "Mom, you can't come back!"

There was no answer, no sign, other than the kitchen faucet dripping and a fly beating at the windowsill.

"Mom, are you here?" Maria asked in a hollow voice. She pounded the table with her fist, and the salt shaker fell over, raining grains of salt.

Angela came into the kitchen. "Who are you talking to?" she asked. "Did Papi come back?"

Maria didn't answer. She stared tenderly at her sister and for a moment thought of hugging her. Instead, she pointed vaguely at the cup of hot chocolate and told her, "It's hot. Be careful not to burn your lips."

Angela walked over to the steaming cup of hot chocolate and, picking it up, turning it around in her small hands and examining it, asked with a smirk on her face, "Have you been using Mama's lipstick?"

"No," Maria said.

"It's all red."

"I didn't use her lipstick. Now, quit it!"

Maria left the kitchen and hurried outside, letting the screen door slam behind her. The sun was dime-bright and hot for early May. The sky was blue and marked with a cargo of white clouds in the east. Mexican music drifted from over the fence from Señor Cisneros's yard.

Maria climbed onto the tire swing that hung from the mulberry and rocked it slowly, her shoes dragging and scraping the dirt under the swing. *Why?* she thought, *why has she come back?* She remembered an argument they had had the day before she died, an argument about Javier, a boy she liked, a boy with green eyes who was always phoning her. Maria bit her lower lip and felt bad about having snapped at her mother.

She looked at their house, which was pink stucco with a runner of green Astroturf on the front steps. She hated that tacky Astroturf, but her father said it wore well, longer than a straw welcome mat.

"Hi," Angela called from the side of the house. She was holding the coffee cup.

Maria turned and looked over her shoulder. She got off the swing and approached her sister.

"You're not done with your chocolate?"

Angela took a sip and smacked her lips, trying to annoy her older sister. "It tastes good."

Maria noticed that Angela's lips were red. She took Angela's chin roughly into her hands and examined her mouth. "Are you wearing Mom's lipstick?"

"No," Angela answered, pushing away hard and almost losing her balance and falling. Some of the chocolate spilled on the front of her blouse. Mad, Angela looked down at the stain. "See what you've done?"

"It's nothing."

"I'm gonna tell Papi when he comes home," she cried,

and stomped off, careful not to spill her remaining hot chocolate.

Maria sat down on the front steps, raking her hand across the Astroturf, thinking of her mother, gone eight days. *What does she want,* she thought to herself. *Should I be nice to Angela? Should I take care of the house?* Mom had never demanded much, but maybe she was asking something now.

When a sparrow swooped and settled on the handrail, Maria jumped to her feet and cried, *"Ay, Dios,"* knowing that a bird was a messenger of death. "What do you want? Get outa here!"

The sparrow locked a gaze on Maria and after a moment of silence flew to the neighbor's roof, then over the house.

Shaken, Maria returned inside the house. Angela, who was in the living room watching television, made a face and said, "I'm gonna tell Papi on you for dirtying my blouse."

Maria passed her without saying anything and went into the kitchen. She looked around slowly as she listened for sounds. The faucet still dripped and the fly now buzzed the overhead light. A ceiling beam creaked, the floor creaked. The water heater in the closet popped and hissed, and the clock on the wall whined its seconds.

It's Mother, she told herself, *she's telling me something.* Maria's gaze fell on her mother's coffee cup on the counter. She walked over and took the cup and poured herself some coffee. She stirred in two spoonfuls of sugar and a splash of milk, and sat down at the small table near the window, her mother's favorite place in the house. She gazed out the window at her mother's garden of tomatoes and chilies, sun-sparking pie tins tied to the vines and banging softly in the breeze.

"What do you want, Mama?" she said after a chill touched her shoulder. "Are you here, Mama? Are you?"

The floor creaked, the ceiling creaked, and the fly that was buzzing the overhead light now beat against the window.

Maria sighed and lowered her gaze on the steam rising from the coffee. She turned the coffee cup around and studied the lipstick marks. She blew on the coffee, raised the cup, and took a sip where the lipstick marks would match her own mouth. Without intending to she moaned in a different voice, her mother's voice, "I'm here and will never leave you, *mi'ja.*"

Maria's hand jumped to her mouth as it tried to keep her mouth from talking. Her hand muffled her dead mother's words, but couldn't stop the words from flowing. Maria ran from the kitchen into the living room, moaning, "I'm here, *mi'ja.*"

Angela was now at the dining table drawing a picture with crayons. She asked, "What did you say?"

Maria moaned through her hand.

"You sound like Mommy," Angela said. She scratched her thigh, swollen with mosquito bites. With her face scrunched up from the pain of scratching, she asked, "How come you got your hands on your mouth?"

Maria's hands tightened around her mouth as words tried to force themselves from the back of her throat.

"See," Angela said, getting down from the chair. "It's a picture of Mommy." Angela raised the picture for her sister to see—a picture of the sisters waving to their mother.

In the drawing their mother was calling, "I'll never leave you, *mi'jas.*"

Maria's mouth twisted with fear. Unable to stop the words, she let her hands flop at her sides and let their mother have her say. Their mother's spirit was circling the house, their lives, with a last good-bye.

About Gary Soto

Gary Soto has written for adults and young readers, and is the author of more than fifteen books, including *The Skirt* and *The Pool Party*. He lives in the Berkeley hills, where he is often kept awake by deer, possums, raccoons, wandering cats, and possibly the footsteps of the motherly ghost that appears in this story.

*Andrew loses his ring—and finds
something amazing. . . .*

Andrew, Honestly

THERESA NELSON

THE RAINSTORM was the last gloomy gasp of an all-around rotten day. Friday the thirteenth, to be exact. Boy, was it ever.

"Rats," Andrew groaned, reeling in his untouched fishing line as the thunder rumbled darkly and the first outsize drops splatted against the bill of his baseball cap. "Wouldn't you know. Well, come on, Trixie; we'd better head back before we get soaked."

Trixie waved her shaggy brown broom of a tail, stood up and stretched, and waited cheerfully for Andrew to gather his gear from the bank of the rushing stream. Trixie didn't mind getting wet. Neither did Andrew, ordinarily, but it was chilly yet for May, and anyhow today had been so crummy that the ominous black clouds—sweeping in out of nowhere, it seemed, swallowing the sun in one depressing gulp—only added to his dismal mood.

It had all started this morning, even before he climbed out of bed, when he opened his eyes and saw his own hand close beside his face on the pillow. It had puzzled him somehow, that hand, though he couldn't think just why, at first: lean and brown it was, just a shade on the grimy side, as always, in spite of an extra-hard scrubbing after last night's worm-digging. But the funny thing was, today there was a peculiar band of clean white skin at the base of the third finger—a perfect half-inch, as purely pale as an Easter lily, that looked as if it hadn't seen the light of day in years and—

"My ring!" Andrew said out loud, sitting bolt upright. "Where's my lucky ring?"

He and Trixie had turned his room upside down then, looking for it. But the ring was nowhere to be found—not under the bed with his broken-apart Erector set or trapped in the sheets with the cracker crumbs or hidden beneath the piles of gum wrappers and race-car tracks and stray socks and wadded-up homework assignments that littered the braided rug. "Shoot," he muttered again and again, plowing his way through the mountain of mess while Trixie barked happily, thinking it was a game, bounding after flying yo-yos and yesterday's underwear. "Where *is* it?"

But the ring was nowhere, nowhere at all, and then of course Andrew's mother had to come in at the worst possible moment to see if he was almost ready for school, so there was *that* scene to be gotten through: "Andrew Dunnigan, what's *happened* in here? I've told you a dozen times this week to clean this room, but this is ridiculous! *Honestly,* Andrew!" And then on top of that he was so late by now that he missed his bus, which put Pop in a foul humor, since it meant he'd have to drive Andrew to school himself and probably be a half hour late for work: *"Honestly, Andrew, sometimes I think you want to get me fired!"* Which was bad enough, but surely not so bad as it was for Andrew, arriving fifteen minutes after the last bell for Mrs. Hitler's fifth-grade social studies class (okay, so her name was Hillister, but you get the picture), just as she was handing back yesterday's quiz: "C-minus, Andrew," she announced through pursed pink lips. "We both know you can do better, if you'll only get your head out of the clouds. Carelessness, Andrew, that's the problem. Just look at this paper," she went on, flaring her nostrils and holding it up for the whole world to see (well, sure, it was filled with scratch-outs and inkblots—he couldn't help it if his pen had exploded—but it didn't *smell* bad or anything). "Was this written by a boy or a chimpanzee? *Honestly,* Andrew!"

"Honestly, Andrew!" Conrad Smith had mimicked in a whisper, as soon as Mrs. Hitler was out of earshot, and everyone had laughed, except pretty Mary Pat Cullen, who blushed and looked sorry, which was even worse.

Oh, it was a rotten day, all right, the low-down doggone type where your tuna-fish sandwich is bound to be soggy (his was) and you lose your milk money through the hole in your pocket (he did) and jam your finger playing softball at recess and never hit the ball once besides and go home feeling about two inches high just to find out your pop has to stay late at work to make up for this morning and can't take you fishing on the lake like he'd promised yesterday so you go by yourself to the stream in the woods but you spend the first hour trying to get your line untangled and of course when you finally do the fish don't bite (did, didn't, did, couldn't, did, did, didn't).

And then it rains.

"It's all on account of that ring, Trixie," Andrew explained miserably, as they trudged through the downpour. "It was the one Uncle David gave me; remember him, Trixie—the old guy with all those great stories and card tricks? Sure you do; he fed you his meat loaf under the table and took me to the circus and never told who it was did that handstand and broke Grandma's crystal thingamabob. And then right before he left he gave me that ring, said he had got it in China from a genuine fortune-teller and I should keep it forever because there was magic in it. And Mom and Pop just laughed, but it was the *truth,* Trixie; else how can you explain a day like this? I've lost all my luck, that's what it is; it's gone, gone, gone. . . ."

Just then there was a flash of lightning, so close by that Andrew could feel the electric heat of it sucking his breath away, and in the same instant came an earsplitting explosion of thunder—*KERBLOOEY!*—that made him yell and jump back, just as a sizzling, blackened half of a tree trunk came crashing down almost at his feet. "Yow!" he shouted. "Good grief, that was close! Trixie, are you all right, girl? Where are you, Trixie?"

He looked around frantically, then to his relief caught sight of a bedraggled brown form tearing through the rain, through the thrashing trees and windswept underbrush— in exactly the wrong direction. "Trixie, where are you going? *That's* not the way!"

But the lightning must have scared her so silly that it

got her homing instincts all turned around, or maybe she was still deaf from the thunder, because she never stopped or even looked back but just kept running and running, so of course all Andrew could do was run after her. And then for a moment he lost sight of her; the rain was as thick as a heavy gray curtain, as loud as a thundering waterfall. Or, no—that was *actual* thunder again, wasn't it? And a *real* waterfall, the one by the ruins of the old Mohegan village. Had they come so far west already? Just then the lightning flashed again, and he saw it clearly: white water crashing into the raging stream, and beside it a limp brown tail disappearing into the cave that gaped in the rocks beneath the fall.

"The cave!" said Andrew, heading for it. "Good girl, Trixie; I should have thought of that myself."

In a few moments he was ducking inside, blinking in the half-light, taking off his cap and shaking the rain from his hair and clothes. Trixie was waiting for him; she barked and jumped up to greet him, adding her muddy paw prints to his soggy T-shirt. "No, Trixie, get down," he began, then sighed and said, "Oh, well, never mind; looks like it's a goner already." He took the shirt off, wrung it out, spread it out to dry on a nice flat rock. Then he picked out another rock for himself and sat down to wait out the storm. Trixie padded around for a bit, sniffing at the trash others had left behind—discarded beer bottles and soda cans, an empty potato-chip bag, somebody's moldy sneakers—and then she came and lay down beside Andrew, putting her head on his knee for petting.

"That's right, girl. We'll just take it easy for a while, that's all. Storm'll be over pretty soon. . . ."

But the rain was coming down harder than ever now, and the lightning was still streaking the sky, the thunder still shaking the earth with its heavy *BOOM*s!

"Don't worry, Trixie; don't you worry, now. . . ."

Was it getting darker?

A skittering noise set Andrew's heart racing, made him jerk his head to the right. Nothing there that he could see; squirrels, most likely, that was all. There were no *bats* in here, were there? Andrew shivered and wished he were home. This cave had always given him the creeps. Not that it was very big, really, or all that mysterious-looking—just a hollowed-out piece of hill where the older guys went sometimes on summer nights to smoke cigarettes and kiss their girlfriends. But Andrew had heard stories—

"Remember the one Uncle David told us, Trixie? About the escaped convict who disappeared out here in the thirties? It was during a storm just like this, you know. The law chased him all the way from Sing Sing, all the way into this cave. And just when they were about to follow him inside, there was this big crash of thunder and lightning that knocked 'em all down. And when they got up he was *gone*, Trixie—vanished into thin air, was all they could figure, 'cause there isn't any other way out, you can see that . . . And then year before last there was all that flap about Suzannah Lambert and Carter Flood, remember? They disappeared, too, right after Iva Ray Lamont saw 'em heading this way. There was a full moon that night, not a cloud in the sky, but Iva Ray swore she heard thunder and strange voices—a kind of chanting, she said, like we heard at school in that filmstrip about the lost Mohegan tribe. . . . Course, Pop says there's a rational explanation for all of it. Suzannah and Carter just eloped, most likely; ten to one they're alive and well and living in Poughkeepsie. And those voices of Iva Ray's—nothing but the wind, or owls, maybe, plus a little imagination. And even the convict—Pop says that lightning must've stunned the lawmen for a minute—knocked 'em out just long enough for that guy to walk right past 'em, easy as pie, so of course he was gone when they came to. But I don't know, Trixie"—Andrew paused, shook his head—"seems like there would have been *tracks* or something; seems like Suzannah would've dropped her mother a postcard, at least. And old Iva Ray—well, she's a nice girl and all but I never heard anyone accuse her of having an imagination. . . ."

It was definitely getting darker. The wind moaned and sent a fresh supply of raindrops spattering against the rocks inside the cave's entrance. Andrew shuddered again, drew closer to his dog. "I'll tell you what Uncle David said, Trixie. He figures this is one of those places where time gets sort of—hung up, some way. Where the fourth dimension has a crack in it, you know? A kind of fault line, maybe, like they have out in California where those underground plates come together. Only, here there's three of 'em—past, present, and future, all rubbing up against each other. And every now and then, when the conditions are just right—like in a thunderstorm, say—there might be a great big *BANG!*—a sort of *timequake,* you know? And then anything—or *anybody*—could slip through: that convict or Suzannah and Carter or a whole gang of Mohegans. Or someone from the future, maybe—some funny-looking guy with little bitty teeth and no muscles except in his button-punching fingers and only eight toes and a big old bald head for his giant-sized brain and huge eyes from watching so much television—"

Trixie lifted her head, cocked her ears. She whined a little.

"Aw, Trixie, I'm only kidding; they're just stories, okay? You know what a joker Uncle David is." Andrew hugged her, and Trixie's ears relaxed again. She put her head back down, and Andrew yawned as he scratched her behind the ears and leaned his own head on the rock shelf behind him. It was covered with new moss, as springy and sweet-smelling as any pillow. He closed his eyes. The sound of rain was steady, soothing. "Nothing but stories, Trixie; don't you worry."

He must have slept for a little while then, because it seemed to him that he was drifting away, floating right out of the cave and up through the raindrops, up high, higher, higher still, over the treetops, over the clouds, as light as any soap bubble. In fact—why, he *was* a bubble, wasn't he? A shining rainbow-colored bubble, more fragile than sea foam. And here above the storm there were hundreds—no, thousands, hundreds of thousands—of other bubbles, bubbles with faces, shifting constantly: now fat, now thin, now short, now tall, beautiful one minute, grotesque the next. Here was a proud Mohegan chieftain, and Suzannah Lambert in a wedding veil, and a scraggly, bearded man with piercing eyes—the convict? Andrew worried. And now here was Uncle David, laughing like always, brighter than all the other bubbles. Only, he was much younger than Andrew remembered, getting younger by the second—or was it that Andrew was getting older? It was impossible to tell. "The ring, Andy!" Uncle David called. "Hold on to the ring!" And Andrew felt terrible, but before he could explain, Uncle David had disappeared, had been replaced by a puzzled-looking gray-haired man. "Come back!" Andrew cried; he was sinking now, slowly but surely, and as he sank he saw that he and all the other bubbles had come from the pipe of an old Chinese fortune-teller, who was sitting on a fat pink cloud, smiling and blowing. Here was a brand-new bubble just appearing: a different sort this time, perfect in every way, as round and golden as—

"My ring!" Andrew shouted. "There's my lucky ring!" But he reached for it too clumsily; when he touched it the bubble burst, shattered in his fingers into a zillion golden splinters.

The fortune-teller shook his head. "Carelessness, Andrew, that's the problem. You've got to get your head out of the clouds." He was frowning now, and the frown was changing his features—to pursed pink lips and flared white nostrils with an odd little piece of black mustache in between. "Are you a boy or a chimpanzee? *Honestly,* Andrew!" And then without warning the fortune-teller jabbed his pipe at Andrew's bubble, and as it exploded around him he could see all the other bubbles popping, too, and hear voices echoing from them in a soapy chorus, *"Honestly!" "Honestly!" "Honestly,* Andrew!" as he plunged like a stone, back through the storm, down through the clouds and the rain and the treetops, down and down and—

KERBLAMMMMM! went the thunder.

Andrew jerked awake, his heart pounding wildly. "Good grief, Trixie, what a nightmare! I was floating and then I was falling and there were all these crazy bubbles and—"

He broke off abruptly. There was a man standing just

inside the mouth of the cave—hardly more than a dark shape, really, silhouetted against the fading gray light that fell uncertainly through the curtain of rain.

"Hello," he said.

"Uh, hi," said Andrew. There was no need to panic, he told himself reasonably, over the thudding of his pulse. *Just some old guy, that's all, caught in the storm same as you.*

"You're—you're Andrew, aren't you?"

Andrew nodded slowly. How did he know his name? Was he a neighbor? Andrew knew most everybody around these parts, but he could be a visitor, maybe; old Mrs. Lambert's brother from the city or—

"Don't you know me?" The stranger sounded puzzled. He took a step or two toward Andrew's rock. Andrew could see him a little more clearly now, but it didn't help much. Although—there *was* something familiar about him; about his eyes, maybe? It was hard to tell in this light. Gray-haired, he was: sixty, at least.

"No, sir, I'm sorry. I mean, I guess I should—?"

"It's okay." The stranger took a step closer. "Maybe . . ." He hesitated, as if he were trying to work something out in his mind. "Maybe you're not supposed to," he finished. He took another step.

Trixie barked. Andrew felt her tense under his hand, ready to spring. "It's okay, girl," he murmured soothingly. "It's okay."

"Trixie?" The man smiled, held out his hand. "Don't *you* know me, girl?"

"No, mister," said Andrew, trying to keep a grip on Trixie's collar. "She might bite; I mean, she's a good dog, really, but she thinks she has to protect me, see, and sometimes with strangers she . . ."

But the man kept coming. "Trixie?" he said again.

"*No,* mister; I'm warning you—"

But it was too late. Trixie bounded out of Andrew's grasp in one mighty lunge. Before he could stop her she was all over the man, leaping up to—

To lick his face?

"But—but she never—" Andrew began as he tried to pull her back. "She *never* likes strangers! *Down,* girl; you'll ruin his suit!"

The man was laughing, hugging her, scratching her behind the ears. "It's all right," he said. "We're old friends, aren't we, girl? Good old Trixie, good dog! Who'd've believed it, after all this time? Oh, it's great to see you, girl!"

Andrew felt a twinge of jealousy. Who *was* this guy, anyhow? Had he been feeding his dog, or what? *"Trixie!* Get *down,* I said."

Trixie looked back at him now, then at the stranger again, and then reluctantly she did as she was told, her tail still wagging like mad.

"I'm sorry, mister," Andrew said stiffly. "I guess she got you all . . ." He paused, confused. *Muddy,* he had been about to say. But there wasn't even one sloppy paw print on the stranger's white shirt, not the first speck of mud on his suit or tie, which were also unaccountably— "Dry," Andrew whispered, his throat suddenly tight. "How can you be dry?"

Another pause. Then, "It's okay, Andy," said the stranger. His smile was gentle, reassuring. "It's a dream, that's all."

Andrew took a step back. His heart was beginning to race again. "Look, if this is some kind of joke—"

"No, no—please—believe me, Andy. It's just a dream, no kidding." The stranger rubbed his eyes, as if he were still trying to get it all straight in his own mind. "I was working late at the office, you see; it's been kind of hectic lately. And I closed my eyes for just a minute; it was raining there too—you know how that sound can get to you. And I must have dozed off, because what came next *had* to be a dream: there were all these—well, I know it sounds crazy, but—there were huge bubbles everywhere, and an old Chinese fortune-teller—"

BOOM! crashed the thunder. *BOOM, CRACKLE, BOOMMMM!*

"Let's get out of here, Trixie!" Andrew hollered, grabbing her by the collar and pulling her out of the cave, into the pouring rain. "He was there—in my nightmare; *that's* where I saw him before!"

They had never run so fast, tearing like mad through the wildly thrashing woods, leaping over fallen branches and newborn streams and pool-sized mud puddles; running, running, regardless of the driving rain, the white-hot lightning flashing all around them, the terrible booming thunder. And at last Andrew's house rose before them in the clearing just ahead; the lights of Andrew's own kitchen windows were shining through the trees—so warm and welcoming that Andrew could have wept with relief. And then he was rushing through his own back door, and his mother's arms were around him—

"Oh, Andy, sweetheart! Thank goodness you're all right! This terrible storm; I was so worried."

106

"Mom, oh, Mom, it was just *awful;* you wouldn't believe! I fell asleep in the cave, and I thought—I mean, I dreamed —this *man*—"

"It's all right, sweetheart; tell me later, when you're dry. Go on upstairs now; hop in the shower before you catch your death. Go on now; up, up! Not you, Trixie; you'll ruin my carpets! Over here on the towels, girl; I'll take care of you."

No shower had ever felt as good. Andrew stood under the warm water for a good fifteen minutes, letting it soothe away the goose bumps, wash away every last trace of the cave and his crazy nightmare. Safe in the steamy bathroom, with everything so real around him—solid blue tile and nubby pink washcloth and little bits of mildew showing on the ceiling where the paint had started to flake (nothing the least bit dreamlike about *mildew,* for Pete's sake) he began to calm down, even to laugh at himself, a little. Dream, shoot! Why, that guy was as real as *he* was— some new neighbor Trixie had made friends with while Andrew was at school, that was all. And he was out walking in the woods when the storm hit, so he had ducked into the cave, same as Andrew. Only, *he* had had sense enough to bring an umbrella; that was why he wasn't wet. In his confusion Andrew just hadn't noticed it, right? Right. As simple as that!

But the dream, said a nagging voice inside his head. *He had the same dream as you, remember?*

Andrew wouldn't listen. There had to be some logical explanation, some dumb coincidence, some trick of memory. He would ask Pop about it; Pop would be able to figure it out. Good old Pop.

He turned off the water then, dried off, and stepped into the pajamas and robe Mom had hung on the rack for him. They were still warm from the dryer, smelling of Cheer.

"Hurry down, Andy!" Mom called from the kitchen as he crossed the upstairs hall to his room. "Supper's ready!"

"Okay, Mom!" he called back, opening his door. "I'll be there in just a—"

"Hello again," said the stranger. He was sitting on the cluttered rug, putting together pieces of race-car track. "I hope I didn't startle you too mu—"

"Aieeeeeeee!" yelled Andrew, slamming the door and racing down the stairs. "Mom! Pop! Come quick—there's a guy—a crazy man or something—I saw him in the woods and now he's upstairs. He's in my room!"

"What?"

"How on earth—?"

"Good Lord, Michael, call the police!"

But Pop had already grabbed a baseball bat and was charging up the stairs, while Andrew and Mom followed with Trixie—who should have been barking her head off, but wasn't.

"Who's there?" yelled Pop, throwing open the door and brandishing the bat high over his head. "Come out, do you hear me?"

The stranger looked up from the rug, startled. And then his eerily familiar eyes widened, and his face broke into a joyful grin. "Oh, my gosh," he said, getting to his feet and opening his arms. "I can't believe it! Is it—is it really you?"

Pop acted as if he hadn't heard a word—or seen anything, even. "I said come out of there! I'm warning you, I'm armed—"

"But he's right *there,* Pop!" said Andrew, pointing. "He's standing right in front of you!"

"Shhh!" said Mom, pulling him back. "Let your father handle this, sweetheart."

"But—"

"Maybe he's hiding in the closet," Pop whispered, jerking his head that way. He crossed the room cautiously—nearly stepping on the stranger's foot in the process—and began banging on the closet door with the bat. "Come out of there!" he shouted. "I'm warning you!"

"But, Pop!" Andrew shouted. "He's *right there*—right *behind* you, don't you see?"

"Whaaa—?" Pop wheeled around, ready to swing away. *"Where?"*

"Right *there*!" Andrew hollered as Trixie walked in calmly and put her head in the stranger's hand for petting. "No, Trixie, stay away from him!"

There was a moment of silence while Pop stood and stared, bat on high, peering past Andrew's pointing finger, straight at the stranger. The only sounds were the rain drumming on the roof, the steady "Heh, heh, heh" of Trixie's dog breath, and Andrew's own pulse, thrumming in his ears. Then—

"Andrew?" Pop said quietly. His eyebrows were arching, the way they always did when he was flustered. "Is this some sort of joke, son?"

Andrew's heart sank. *"Joke?"* he repeated weakly, too stunned to believe his own ears. "But don't you—I mean, he's right *there*!"

"I don't think he can see me, Andy," said the stranger. He shook his head, as if he were . . . disappointed? "Or hear me either."

"But that's—that's impossible," Andrew stammered. "*I* can see you."

"I tried to tell you before," said the stranger. He sounded apologetic. "Back at the cave, remember? I'm dreaming, you see; you're in my dream and—"

"No!" Andrew put his hands over his ears. "I don't want to hear!"

"Andrew." Pop's voice was stern now. "This isn't funny, son." He lowered the bat, dropped it on the floor with the rest of the mess. "I don't know what kind of game you're playing, but I'm not in the mood, do you hear me? Not after the day I've had."

"But—"

Pop held up his hand for silence. "*No more,* young man. Not another word." He started across the room again, and for a second Andrew thought he would surely run right into the stranger. Good, he thought; at least that would prove *something.* But instead, when he reached him there was a peculiar sort of shimmering, as if the stranger were made of water or light, and Pop passed right through him without even blinking, while Andrew stood and gaped. "I suggest you apologize to your mother for scaring her half to death," Pop said as he passed him, and then he walked out into the hall and down the stairs.

Andrew sank down on his bed, still too flabbergasted to speak. Was he going crazy?

"Andy, honey," said Mom, sitting down beside him and putting an arm around his shoulders, "what were you thinking? Oh, I know you were only teasing, sweetheart, just trying to make us laugh, but—well, it's not a good day, that's all, with all the trouble at work, and then we were so worried with you out in the storm . . ."

"I'm sorry," the stranger said gently. He was looking at Andrew's mother. "It's my fault. I guess I came at a bad time."

"No kidding," Andrew muttered, glaring at him.

But Mom thought Andrew was speaking to *her*. "*Excuse* me?" she said, with that hurt sound in her voice. "What was that, Andrew?"

"No, Mom, not you; I was talking to—to Trixie, that's all," Andrew said hastily.

His mother's brow wrinkled. "Hmm," she said, putting a hand on his forehead. "You're not feverish, are you? Catching cold, I'll bet. All right, young man"—she stood up briskly, began turning back the bedspread—"you just climb under the covers now; that's my prescription. I'll bring your supper up on a tray."

"But—"

"No, sir, no arguments. What you need is a good night's rest."

And then she was gone, closing the door behind her, and Andrew was left alone with the stranger. Or not *quite* alone; there was Trixie, too, good old Trixie, at least—even if she *had* forgotten whose dog she was. "C'mere, girl," said Andrew. She hesitated for a moment, as if she were still confused, looking from one to the other.

"Go on, Trixie," said the stranger. That did the trick; she walked over to the bed, jumped on it, and curled up beside Andrew.

111

For some reason tears sprang to his eyes. "So how come *she* can see you?" asked Andrew, blinking them back.

"I don't know," said the stranger. "I guess—well, I guess animals just have sharper senses. And Trixie was always something special, weren't you, girl?" He reached out to stroke her head, then saw Andrew's expression and hesitated. "Look, Andy," he said, "I'm really sorry about all this confusion. I never meant to cause you trouble."

He looked so apologetic, so really, truly sorry, that Andrew almost forgot to be afraid—and mad, and jealous, and hurt. The guy had pretty good manners for a—a *whatever* the heck he was; you had to give him that, anyway. Andrew sighed. "Forget it," he said. "It's only a dream, right?"

"Right!" said the stranger, lighting up again. "Amazing, isn't it? This whole place, I mean—the woods and the stream, the cave and waterfall—why, they haven't changed a bit! And this great old house—well, they just don't make 'em like this anymore, that's all." He paused once more, looked around him, smiling. "Amazing," he repeated softly. "This room—the detail of it! Who'd've thought I'd remember these tiny decals on the race cars? Or these old tic-tac-toe games scratched into the headboard, or this funny patchwork quilt with the rip you have to hide under the pillow; why, I haven't thought of any of it in years! And just look here—there are even *cracker* crumbs, do you see? I mean, it all seems so real!"

Andrew sat up straight. "What do you mean, *seems* real? Look, mister, this is *my* room, see? And this is *my* dog, and *my* bedspread, and I'm the one who ate the crackers and *left* the crumbs, don't you get it? And you're . . . well, I

112

don't know who you are, or *what* you are, but you're definitely *not* real. My pop walked straight *through* you, remember? No, sir, if anybody's dreaming here, it must be me, that's all. And any minute I'll wake up and you'll be gone and that'll be just *fine* with me—" Andrew broke off suddenly, as a terrible thought struck him. "Unless . . ."

"Unless what?" asked the stranger. He was leaning in, interested.

Andrew didn't answer right away. Wind groaned, thunder rattled. "Unless you're dead," Andrew whispered. He was thinking of all those movies and TV shows he had seen —about ghosts who didn't *know* they were dead, getting stuck on earth forever and ever. . . .

"Dead?" The stranger looked shocked. "Good grief, I *hope* not." He put his hand to his heart, checking. After a moment his face cleared. "Still beating," he said. *"That's* a relief. No, no, I couldn't possibly be dead. Unless . . ."

"Unless what?"

"Unless—well, you don't suppose this is heaven, do you?"

"Heaven?" Now it was Andrew's turn to look shocked. "Good grief, I *hope* not! I mean, there's *homework* here, you know? And lawns to mow and cauliflower on Tuesdays and red bugs and deer ticks and Conrad Smith; he's a guy in my class who—"

"Who shoots you in the behind with his pellet gun and sticks his bubble gum inside your locker and throws your best lunches out the bus window," the stranger finished for him, nodding sympathetically. "Oh, yeah," he said, "I almost forgot."

113

Andrew's mouth was hanging open. "How'd you *know* all that?"

But before the stranger could answer, the door opened and Pop came in, bringing a tray with supper on it: chicken pot pie and applesauce and carrot sticks and a tall glass of milk. "Hungry, son?"

"Sure, Pop," said Andrew, even though his stomach had so many knots in it that he wasn't, really. But he knew that this was Pop's way of apologizing for having lost his temper earlier—that he'd never say it in so many words but would sit with him and talk instead about what to do for a jammed finger and the Mets' chances of signing that hot young third baseman from Miami and whether or not the fish might be biting on the lake tomorrow once this rain let up. Which he did . . . and all the time he was talking the stranger was watching him with the oddest expression on his face—half glad, half sad—as if *he* were the one who was hungry, somehow. It deepened when Pop said goodnight: "New day tomorrow, right, Captain? You have a good rest now. Don't forget to brush your teeth." And when Mom joined them for her good-night kiss: "Feeling better, sweetheart? Don't forget your prayers. . . ."

And then the door was closing again. The stranger was quiet, staring at it. "Maybe not heaven," he said at last. "But it was home."

"Home?" Goose bumps tiptoed up Andrew's spine again. "I don't understand. . . ."

The stranger just looked at him for a moment. "Sure you do," he said. And suddenly Andrew knew why those eyes were so familiar. Not just from the nightmare, but from his own mirror. "No," he murmured. "That's impossible."

"Nothing's impossible in a dream."

Andrew thought this over. And then he said, "But—you're not planning on *staying*, are you? I mean, is it so terrible, where you come from?"

"Oh, no!" The stranger was smiling now. "I—you—we like it just fine. My son—he's terrific. He reminds me a little of Pop, you know? And my grandson—he likes to fish too. But things have been so hectic lately, we haven't had a chance. . . ."

"So you *do* want to go back," said Andrew. *That* was a relief, anyway.

"Oh, yes," said the stranger. "Of course. Only . . ."

"Only what?"

"Only I'm not quite sure how to go about it. Waking up, I mean."

"But that's easy, isn't it? You just open your eyes, that's all."

The stranger shook his head. "I tried that already, when you were so upset, you know. I didn't want to intrude."

"And it didn't *work*? Good grief! Well, you'll just have to try again, that's all."

The stranger paused for a moment, as if he were concentrating very hard. Then he sighed. "It's no good. Something seems to be holding me back."

"So what are we supposed to do now?"

"I don't know," said the stranger. He rubbed his eyes. "It seems to me that this has all happened before. But it was so long ago; I can't remember how it turns out. I've tried, but—no luck."

"Good grief," said Andrew. Luck again—that was the whole problem, wasn't it? "My ring," he said under his breath. "If only I hadn't lost that ring!"

"Ring? What ring?"

Andrew sighed. "My lucky ring. I can't find it anywhere. I've looked and looked, but it's disappeared."

The stranger was fishing in his pocket. "Is this the one you mean?" he asked, pulling out his hand and holding it open for Andrew to see what was inside: a small golden circle, set with a polished black stone—

"My ring!" Andrew cried. "Where'd you get it?"

"From my uncle David," said the stranger. "He brought it to me from China, and he told me—"

"To keep it forever," Andrew finished breathlessly, "because there was magic in it."

"Right," said the stranger. He was grinning now. It made him look—like a kid again. "And so I've always kept it—on my finger, at first, then in my pocket, when it grew too small. And in all these years I only lost it once."

"When you were my age," Andrew whispered.

"Exactly," said the stranger, handing it to him.

"And where did you—I mean, where will I—find it?" Andrew asked, turning it over lovingly in his fingers.

"It was my father who found it," said the stranger, "while he was fixing a leak in the pipe under the bathroom sink. The ring was caught in the trap, you see; it had slipped off while I was washing my hands."

"So *that's* where it went!" Andrew exclaimed. He thought back to last night; well, of course—in all that lather he'd never even noticed!

"That's where it went," said the stranger. "I remember now. I remember everything."

"Everything? You mean—"

"How it all turns out." The stranger held out his hand. "I'll need the ring again, if you don't mind. I have to put it on for the magic to work."

"But you said it's too small," said Andrew, reluctantly handing it over.

"I think I can still get it on my pinkie," said the stranger, pushing hard. "There, you see? Not bad at all."

"Now what?"

"Now I go back to the cave. Before the storm is over." He looked out the window. The rain was still coming down, but a bit of moon had found a rent in the clouds. It shone right through the stranger; for a moment he seemed to be made of moonlight.

"Will you be all right?" Andrew asked. "Should I go with you?"

"You're always with me," said the stranger. "But for now you're supposed to stay here. You'll go to sleep. And I'll wake up. And then . . ."

"Then what?" asked Andrew, lying back on the pillows. He was suddenly terribly sleepy.

"Then I'll take tomorrow off, I think. Go fishing with my grandson, maybe." The moonlight wavered, blurring the stranger's outline. Trixie looked up, whimpered a little. "Good-bye, Trixie," he said, scratching her behind the ears. "Good-bye, old girl."

He was fading fast now, smiling at Andrew. "Did I tell you? My grandson—they named him Andy."

"For me?" asked Andrew.

"For us," said Andrew.

Morning. Not just any old morning, either: *Saturday* morning, fresh washed by the storm, drenched in sunshine and birdsong.

"What a crazy night, Trixie," said Andrew, sitting up and stretching. "You wouldn't believe the dreams I had. . . ."

"Good morning, son," said Pop, putting his head in at the door. "Perfect weather for the lake, don't you think? Better grab a bite to eat before we go. Mom's making pancakes."

Andrew was downstairs in under a minute, Trixie at his side.

"Sleep well, sweetheart?" asked Mom as she filled his plate. "That was some storm, wasn't it? All sorts of strange things in the air."

"Strange things? What strange things?"

"Oh, well, it was on the radio this morning; I couldn't believe my ears. Talking about some crazy man in an old-fashioned prison uniform—police found him wandering around on the edge of town, mumbling something about Sing Sing. He wanted to turn himself in, he said; he'd seen enough of the 1990s. . . . And then Helen Lambert called, just overjoyed—seems Suzannah turned up on her doorstep in the middle of the night—just walked in with that boyfriend of hers, saying they were married now. Been staying with friends all this time, apparently; Helen says she's brought some of them with her. Native Americans, I think she said; they don't seem to speak any English. I forget now—what was it she called them?"

"Mohegans," Andrew breathed.

"Why, yes!" said Mom. "How'd you know?"

But before he could answer, Pop was calling to him from the top of the stairs: "Run and get me my toolbox, will you, Andy? I'd better get this taken care of before we go. Looks like we've got a leak under the sink."

"Sure, Pop!" Andrew called back, already on his feet. "Be right there." He looked at Trixie, who smiled her widest dog smile and wagged her tail. "Did you hear that, girl? The sink is leaking!"

It was going to be a wonderful day.

About Theresa Nelson

I love storms. I grew up near the Texas Gulf Coast—far enough inland to be safe from the brunt of the most dangerous weather, but close enough that I can remember wild nights when the streets would flood and the electricity would go out and all eleven of us children would gather around my parents in the candle-lit living room. "Tell us a story," we would beg as the lightning flashed and the thunder rolled and the wind lashed the rain against the taped-up windows. "A scary story." Why we actually *enjoyed* being frightened out of our wits is still a mystery to me, but Mama and Daddy—storm and story lovers, both —never failed us. "It was a dark and stormy night," one of them would begin. And we were hooked.

There are storms of one kind or another in all my books. In *The 25¢ Miracle* Elvira runs away during a torrential Texas downpour. In *Devil Storm* (based on one of my mother's true stories) Tom the Tramp struggles to save the Carroll family from the most monstrous hurricane ever to hit North America. Midway through *And One for All* a snowstorm transforms Geraldine's world, while far away in Vietnam her brother Wing must face another, fiercer storm. And in my latest novel, *The Beggars' Ride* (set on the boardwalk in Atlantic City, New Jersey), the game of survival that Cowboy's gang is playing takes a terrifying twist one dark and stormy night. . . .

I've recently moved with my husband and our three sons to Los Angeles, California, rightly famous for its sunshine. But no sooner had I sat down at my typewriter to hunt for ghosts than the clouds were gathering—in my mind's eye, anyway—and I found myself back at the wonderful old farmhouse in Westchester County, New York, where we once lived. (It's a haunting house—not *haunted*, exactly, but haunting in the way it has stayed with me, even in my dreams.) And there was my youngest son, dodging raindrops. He was himself—and not himself at all; younger and older all at once. Which set me wondering: What if this was no ordinary storm? What if it was a sort of cosmic disturbance that altered time and space, gave substance to dreams, made it possible for a person to trespass on his own history? And so I followed Andrew into the woods, past the trout stream and the waterfall and into the ancient cave beneath, just to see what might happen.

I could have sworn I heard thunder.

Theresa Nelson's first novel, *The 25¢ Miracle,* was a 1986 *School Library Journal* Best Book of the Year and the winner of the Washington Irving Children's Choice Award. *Devil Storm* was chosen as an NCSS–CBC Notable Children's Trade Book in the Field of Social Studies. *And One for All* was named an ALA Notable Children's Book, an ALA Best Book for Young Adults, a *School Library Journal* Best Book of the Year, an NCSS–CBC Notable Children's Trade Book in the Field of Social Studies, and an International Reading Association Teachers' Choice. It was included in *Booklist*'s Editors' Choice, the *American Bookseller* Pick of the Lists, and *The Horn Book*'s Fanfare. Ms. Nelson's most recent novel is *The Beggars' Ride,* a *School Library Journal* Best Book of 1992, which was also honored in *Fanfare* and selected by the American Library Association as both a Notable Children's Book and a Best Book for Young Adults.

Gone, but not forgotten. . . .

Grandmother's Ghost, the Gilded Bathroom, and Other Home Improvements

BARBARA ANN PORTE

I THINK GRANDMA would not have come back after she died had Tata not taken it into her head to move back into Grandmother's house, knock out some walls, and install a wet bar, a walk-in closet, plus a gilded commode with a sink and a sauna to match. Other home improvements included central air-conditioning, an upscale kitchen, and a large electric bed that gave massages. This was not Grandmother's style. Family members warned my aunt.

"Some things a person *can* do, but they're liable not to turn out in her own best interest," Daddy, Tata's older brother, said.

"You're planning to do what?" her oldest sibling, Henny Penny, asked. Henny Penny is not my aunt's real name, of course. Her real name is Henrietta Martina, but no one in this family ever calls her that. Only Uncle Bo, the youngest one, said nothing.

"He's probably speechless," Daddy told me. I myself was rather shocked at so many changes in such a short time. Of course, it was nothing to the way I felt later, after the walls had actually come down, and the plaster was all swept away, and the smallest bedroom had become a closet, and the bathroom fixtures glittered in place, against red-and-gold wallpaper, and Tata had fully assembled her mechanical bed. That was when Grandmother moved back in with us.

"Reclaimed her residence" was how Daddy put it, and meant from Tata and me. Daddy lived at home. The reason I didn't live there with him was because Grandmother's house was within walking distance of the school I wanted to attend. Also, Daddy traveled sometimes on business and didn't like leaving me alone overnight. My mother was gone, having taken off one day with no warning.

"It's time for me to pursue my own life as a painter," she said, speaking long distance from California. I did not plan to visit her there, and for more reasons than only earthquakes.

"I have my own life to pursue too," I told her on the telephone. Of course, when I said it, I wasn't planning on pursuing it with Grandmother's ghost looking over my shoulder.

"Don't think I don't know what you are up to," Grandma had often told me when she was alive, and I was still living at home with my own parents. When she died, though I sorrowed greatly, I felt certain I was through with the watching part. But, see, I was wrong, though I do think in this case it was Tata whose actions most called for scrutiny. Weren't all the home improvements her idea? One by one her siblings came to see them.

"Funny commode," said Uncle Bo, and shook his head.

"That's some bed" was all Daddy said, an understatement even for him. Aunt Henny Penny looked around carefully.

"How interesting," she told Tata, sounding doubtful. She herself wasn't too keen on most things electric, frequently running into problems with appliances of her own. I thought perhaps it came from her having too many.

"It comes from never reading the inserts that come with them," Aunt Tata said. She was a careful reader of instructional manuals, and capably handled all things mechanical.

"I've no experience, though, with ghosts," she said, complaining to her sister.

"Well, of course you don't," Aunt Henny Penny answered kindly, looking in the mirror, adjusting her hat. "Still, it seems sort of cozy to have Mother back." Tata glared at her.

"Sure it seems cozy to you," she grumbled. "Mother didn't move into your house. She's moved in with us."

This was how we knew it: She rustled things. She bustled through the air. Now and then she bumped against a wall, or ceiling. It was good for us we could not see her. Grandmother in real life was nearly six feet tall, with wild silver braids, and cinnamon skin. She had long fingernails she polished bright red. I think we would have jumped out of our skins if her ghost had come back visible.

As it was, we only had to get used to the noise. She frequently dropped things, scouring powder in the gilded bathroom, for instance, or soapy water on the kitchen floor. Sometimes she startled others, and caused them to drop things. Tata, for instance, had broken many a bar glass that way.

"Well, that's the last of my stemware," she told Henny Penny, sweeping glass shards into a dustpan.

"Mother may be trying to tell you something," Aunt Henny Penny said on her way out the door, pausing to kiss us both good-bye. I thought she was quite likely right. Grandmother had always disapproved of anything at all alcoholic, including rum cake. She'd always believed in sanitized bathrooms and floors kept immaculate.

"See, that's what housekeepers are for," Tata said. Finding one, however, turned out to be much easier than keeping one. Housekeepers, we soon discovered, didn't care to work in haunted houses.

"It isn't haunted. It's only Mother," Tata told the third and last one.

"Ummm-hummm. You call it what you like, but let me tell you something. You can have gilded tubs, keypad kitchens, and three-speed beds, but ghosts go back a long time, and they're not about to be run off by something electric." She was running off herself that moment, finally undone by an empty pie pan that had jumped off the counter and clattered angrily across the kitchen floor, all on its own steam as far as anyone could tell.

Tata blamed Daddy. "It's your fault," she said. He'd

stopped by to say hi, then stayed on to finish the pie. It was a sweet-potato pie. Daddy loved sweet-potato pie. Well, Grandmother loved sweet-potato pie too.

"See, Mother probably wanted a slice. No doubt she was ticked off considerably to find you'd eaten it all."

Daddy protested. "I didn't eat it all. It was already half gone when I got here." Though that was true, the words were hardly out of his mouth when the pan resumed its rattling, banging, and clattering in place on the floor.

"I think Grandmother's trying to tell you something," I said. She'd always hated seeing her children argue. I hated it too.

"We're not arguing. We're just discussing," they always said, and made up quickly. They made up now.

"See, it's really your fault. Your pies are too good." Daddy stood and kissed his sister. Then he kissed me, too, and went on home.

That night Tata began planning her homecoming party. It was an annual affair. Tata's parties were famous. She was an excellent cook and an extravagant hostess, also highly entertaining. Plus she played pinochle like a river gambler. Well, so did Grandma, and all Tata's siblings, but they never came to her parties.

"Too late and too loud," all of them said, and meant by the time her parties started, they were ready for bed, and also they preferred soft music. I never went to her parties either. I was always too young.

"Well, you're older now, and living with me, plus I could use a hand with the serving," Tata said, and meant minus a housekeeper, she needed my help. We spent the next several days drawing up check sheets of groceries and paper supplies to buy, and things to do to get ready. Tata telephoned her invitations. She took out last year's guest list. Almost everyone she had known since kindergarten was on it. She added some names, and crossed out one. Dr. Ted McGarrity wasn't to come.

"Dr. Ted's trouble," Tata said. "Who knows whom he'd bring, or what they would do when they got here." Grandma had told her that for years, but she'd never listened. Then last month we saw his picture in the newspaper. *Local doctor implicated in phony-prescriptions and imported-drugs ring* was the caption. "That's one headache I don't need," Tata said as she drew a line through his name. Tata's parties may have been a bit on the wild side, but nothing illegal ever went on in her house, and certainly wasn't about to in Grandma's.

When homecoming weekend arrived, we were ready. Containers of homemade potato and macaroni salads filled the refrigerator. Hot chicken wings were ready for frying. Slow-cooked beans and greens and open-pit barbecue filled Tata's pots, just needing reheating. Biscuit dough had been rolled and pies had been baked. Glass dishes on card tables held honey-roasted peanuts, cashews, and pretzels. Fancy new glasses were lined up in rows on the wet bar, alongside ice buckets, fruit punch, mulled apple cider, soda pop, beer, and champagne. Balloons, streamers, and banners hung from ceilings, windows, and walls. The house looked very festive, and so did I.

By five I was already dressed. I had on new silver-studded jeans, a beaded blouse with fringes, and a half dozen bangles on each wrist. "You look perfect for serving," said

127

Tata, still wearing her work clothes and an old headwrap. She planned to take a nap before she showered and dressed. Her new hostess gown hung on a well-padded hanger, suspended from a closet door hook. It was red to the floor, speckled in gold, with a very deep neckline.

"Hey, you match the commode," Uncle Bo had told her several weeks ago, when he saw it.

"Did someone ask you?" Aunt Tata retorted. But after he'd gone, she inspected herself in her new bathroom mirror. "I guess I do too," she said, laughing, then admired her new bathroom fixtures. She could hardly wait to show off all her home improvements to her friends. She hummed to herself the whole time she was dressing.

By half past nine her guests began arriving. Some came in fancy cars. Some carried food. I took more than one honey-cured ham into the kitchen; also pans of corn bread, pots of baked beans, and a large bucket of curried goat. By midnight the house was full. Glittering people in beautiful clothing were talking and laughing, dancing and singing, eating and drinking, and some playing pinochle. In every corner friends told stories and remembered way back when. I scurried around with trays of food. That was when the doorbell rang. Tata went to see who was there. I wondered who could possibly still be missing, or would come so late. I hoped maybe Daddy had changed his mind and decided to join us. Or maybe Henny Penny, or Uncle Bo. But, no, it wasn't any one of them. Aunt Tata had barely cracked open the door when a very large foot was shoved in.

"That's what peepholes are for," I thought I heard somebody say in a whisper that sounded like Grandma's. Then a very large hand pushed the door open, and I gasped at the view of Dr. Ted McGarrity coming through, all six foot four of him, with a buddy as tall on either side. They wore black suits and boots; and wide brightly colored ties. One had on a cowboy hat. They were carrying brown bottles and jugs of homemade concoctions and unlabeled brews. They pushed aside the cider and punch bowls, and set what they carried down on the bar.

"Hey sister, we've come to party," said Dr. Ted, and flashed a grin that didn't look friendly. His buddies grinned too. They looked like a trio of sharks who'd been at a party too many already that night.

"Not in my house. Take my advice, and get out," Aunt Tata told him. Uselessly she tried pushing him with both hands toward the door. He jeered at her, unbudging.

"Who's going to make me?" he asked.

"You just watch me," Tata said. Then she stomped past him, her cheeks burning, heading for the kitchen telephone. Before she even could press nine, Ted tackled her from behind and wrestled the receiver from her hands.

"You and who else?" he asked.

While this was going on, I tried to slip away to use the telephone in the bedroom, but found my path blocked by one of Ted's buddies. "I don't think you want to do that. You're such a cute little girlie, it would be a shame to see you get hurt." Then he reached out one huge fist, laid it against my jaw, moved it downward to my chin, and kept going. That's when everything started.

"Ouch," yelled the buddy, and pulled back his hand as though he'd been burned. He looked at it, I think, more in astonishment than in pain. Even so, I could see a blister was definitely forming. Then a chill wind from nowhere blew through the house, and curtains waved wildly though all the windows were closed. Bar bottles and glasses crashed to the floor, and a dish towel flew through the air and wrapped itself around Ted's eyes like a blindfold. The salads, mulled cider, and punch bowls turned over. Pieces of honeyed ham and curried goat seemed everywhere. Only the guests remained as they were, as though frozen in place, wide-eyed and staring. Aunt Tata was smiling. It took me three seconds, then I understood why.

"I want you out of my house now, and so does my mother, and *we're* going to make you," Aunt Tata said, jubilant, watching Dr. Ted McGarrity unwind his blindfold.

"Your mother?" said Dr. Ted, starting to grin. See, he *still* didn't get it. But the next minute he did. There was a loud report like a gun going off. I thought at first it was thunder, but Ted and his buddies knew a gun when they heard one. It was Grandmother's old rifle she'd kept locked in her closet, unused for years, to guard against poisonous snakes.

"More bad luck. What an inconvenient thing to have happen," said Ted, and just that quick he was gone, taking his buddies along. The party went on until it was morning. There were no further mishaps.

"Well, if that Ted McGarrity isn't a low-down poisonous snake I don't know who is, and so are his buddies," Aunt Tata said afterward, dusting off Grandma's rifle and locking it back in the closet. For all I know, it's still there. Ted and his buddies never came back, and neither did anyone else ever come bother us after that. Word got around fast.

Grandmother stayed on, and we came to take comfort in her creaking sounds, and found her presence cozy. This was the best part:

"I want you to stop that now, and so does my grandmother" was all I had to say from then on to put an end to anyone's evil behavior.

"See, such is the power of a story," Uncle Bo told me.

"It goes to show a person should never go anywhere uninvited," Daddy explained. Aunt Henny Penny saw it this way:

"Home improvements can be fine in their place, but old-time ways are often the best. What saved this family in the end wasn't something electric."

When I heard all this, I knew they were right. That my grandmother's love could be so strong is the tale I have handed down.

About Barbara Ann Porte

Barbara Ann Porte has written many books for children, and also stories for adults. Among her recent titles are: *Ruthann and Her Pig* and *Fat Fanny, Beanpole Bertha, and the Boys*, both published by Orchard Books; also *Taxicab Tales, a Turkey Drive, and Other Tales*, as well as the Harry books (*Harry's Dog, Harry in Trouble, Harry Gets an Uncle* . . .), all published by Greenwillow. She lives in Virginia, and comments as follows about her own work: "The idea that relatives, and friends, I love can die and disappear is almost more than I can bear. I sometimes write to bring them back and keep them by my side. The ghost story in this anthology was, in part, just such an effort."

A lesson from beyond?

The Fifth-Grade Ghost

JOHANNA HURWITZ

ELIOT PARKS was a so-so student. Although he could have been just as smart as anyone else in the fifth grade, he was lazy. Frequently he neglected to bring his books home from school. Then it was impossible for him to do his homework. Eliot just shrugged his shoulders. "I'll do it next time," he promised his teacher. But each time there was another excuse.

Most school subjects bored Eliot. The only thing that roused his interest was a small section in the school library where he had discovered books on supernatural or unexplainable phenomena. Eliot read all he could find about Bigfoot, the Abominable Snowman, the Loch Ness monster, the Bermuda Triangle, and things like that. He didn't really believe in ghosts and the supernatural, but mysteries of that sort were a thousand times more interesting than fifth-grade social studies or arithmetic.

On the first Tuesday in February, Mrs. Wheatley collected the page of math problems that she had assigned to her students as homework. Eliot opened his notebook and looked for the worksheet the teacher had given the class the day before. It was silly of him even to pretend to get the sheet, because as usual he hadn't bothered to take his books home with him. He knew the sheet was just as blank as it had been the day before when he had stuck the page inside his notebook. Still, he riffled through his papers, just like everyone else. To his amazement, when he located the page he discovered that it was not blank at all. Every answer had been filled in. Eliot knew he hadn't done it. Someone else must have accidentally filled in his sheet, he thought as he examined it. The weird thing was that his name was written on the top of the sheet. It even looked like his handwriting. But unless his memory was playing tricks on him, Eliot was sure that he had not done the homework. Then he noticed a small piece of yellow paper stuck onto the reverse side.

Eliot removed the yellow paper. It was from one of those little pads that had pages which could stick to other pieces of paper. Mrs. Wheatley had a pad like that but her pad was white and it had a border of smiley faces on it. This was just plain yellow. There were words on the paper. It said, *Doesn't it make you feel good to be able to hand in your homework on time?*

Eliot's face turned bright red. Someone was playing a joke on him. His seatmate, Grace Ann Connolly, was turning pages in her notebook. There was no way she would have done the homework for him. He looked around the room. Everyone was handing in their work. No one was looking at him. Eliot crumpled the yellow note and stuck it in his pocket.

Mrs. Wheatley reached for his page of homework. She smiled at him. "Eliot. Good for you. I'm glad to get this," she said. Eliot handed her the paper, but he did not respond. Afterward he thought to himself that it had been stupid of him to hand in the sheet. Whoever had written that message and filled in the answers for him had probably put in all the wrong ones to get him in trouble. Better not to get any grade than to get a bad one.

Mrs. Wheatley marked the homework sheets while her students were in phys ed. Later, when she returned them to the students, Eliot was amazed to see that his page was covered with bright red check marks. He certainly hadn't expected that. On the bottom of the page Mrs. Wheatley had written in bright red letters, *Keep up the good work!* Eliot was confused. He didn't know if he should be pleased or not by what had happened.

"How many did you get right?" asked Grace Ann Connolly. She was kind of cute, but she had the annoying habit of chewing on a piece of her long blond hair.

Eliot could see a couple of crosses on her page.

"All of them," he said smugly. The whole thing was just like magic.

At three o'clock when the class was dismissed for the day, Eliot wondered if he ought to take his books home. There had been a new sheet of assigned arithmetic problems and a sheet with questions about their science unit too. Although he had watched his classmates carefully, he still didn't have a clue in the world about who had done his work for him. He had even gone to the boys' room to study the little yellow note, which he had hidden in his pocket. The words were printed in green ink. He couldn't recognize who had written them. He didn't know of anyone in his class who had a pen that wrote green.

Eliot didn't know if he should risk having someone fooling around with his papers. Next time they might get him in trouble. But he made up his mind to live dangerously. He was curious to see if this mysterious homework spirit would appear again. He liked the idea of having his own private invisible pal secretly doing his homework for him.

On Wednesday morning Eliot didn't even wait for Mrs. Wheatley to ask for the homework. As soon as he was in his seat, he reached into his desk for his loose-leaf book. He pulled out the homework sheets and to his delight, again, both were filled in. Whoever was doing his homework had again managed to make the writing on the science sheet look just like Eliot's. It was quite amazing. Then Eliot turned the sheets over.

On the arithmetic sheet there was a little yellow note. It said, *How will you ever pass the quiz next week if you don't do this yourself?* Eliot pulled the paper off and crumpled it up. Then he turned over the science paper. *I would have thought that this is a subject that would interest you. Why don't you give it a chance?* the writing on the yellow note said. Eliot handed in the sheets with his classmates. But all day long he kept thinking about the words on them. Something strange was going on in his class and he didn't understand it at all.

"Did you do your homework last night?" he asked his classmate, Brian Prince. Brian was another kid, like Eliot, who didn't always complete the assignments on time.

"Yeah," said Brian. "Lately I started doing them. It's kinda fun. The arithmetic is like doing a puzzle, once you understand how to do it." Brian paused a moment and licked his lips. "Eliot?" he said.

"Yeah?" asked Eliot.

"Do you believe in magic? Or ghosts?"

"Ghosts? You got to be kidding," said Eliot. Brian was no help to him at all.

"So when did you start doing your homework?" he asked his classmate. He thought Brian was a goof-off like him.

"A few weeks ago," said Brian.

Eliot decided that he wasn't going to let a yellow piece of paper bully him into doing his homework. So that day he again left his books and papers at school when he went home. But during the afternoon he asked his mother for some money.

"If you've spent all your allowance, then you have to wait till Friday," she said.

"This is important," pleaded Eliot. "I want to buy a special kind of notepad for school."

"School supplies?" said his mother. "That's different." She gave Eliot a dollar and he ran off to the local candy store, which also sold stationery supplies. Eliot didn't even look at the candy bars or chewing gum displayed in the front of the store. He went straight to the back, where the notebooks and pens and markers were sold. There, on a rack, next to the mending tape, he saw just what he wanted. He took down a small blue pad of the sticky note-paper. He wanted to write a couple of messages to the person or thing that was doing his homework. It occurred to him to wonder where his mysterious creature had acquired the yellow pad of sticky notes. Did they have stationery supply stores in outer space?

Once again on Thursday, Eliot found completed homework sheets waiting in his notebook. One yellow note said, *This only took ten minutes to do. How can you be so lazy that you won't devote ten minutes to a little homework?* The second note said, *Whatever you want to be when you grow up, you'll need to know a little something. At the rate you are going, your brain is going to atrophy.*

Eliot sat staring at the sheets. He didn't know what the word *atrophy* meant. He'd have to look it up in the dictionary later on. He was sure it wasn't good. But right now he had something to do. He stuck several little blue notes into his notebook. Two could play this game. He had written a message on each blue note. *Who are you?* he asked. *Are you a kid in this class? Or are you some kind of a ghost or something?*

On another note he wrote, *Why should I do my homework if you're so good at doing it for me?* And finally, on the last note, he wrote, *Can I meet you? What do you look like?*

Thursday was about the longest day in Eliot's life. It was longer than the day before Christmas or the day before his birthday. He couldn't wait for it to be over and for Friday to come. He wanted to see if there would be any yellow notes to answer his questions. He was startled, however, to receive the marked homework sheets back from Mrs. Wheatley. "You didn't do as well today as you did the last couple of days," she told him when she returned his arithmetic homework. Eliot looked and noticed that there were only two checks. All his other answers were wrong. He looked over the paper. No wonder. The stupid ghost who was doing his homework didn't know the nine times table. There were some really dumb mistakes.

"I got them all right today," Grace Ann reported to Eliot.

"So what?" said Eliot. He was annoyed that the ghost had let him down. When Grace Ann wasn't looking, he pulled his little blue pad out of his pocket and wrote another note. *How come you messed up the nine times table? Are you stupid or something?*

The homework that evening wasn't a worksheet. The students had to bring in their book reports. Mrs. Wheatley had given them that assignment two weeks ago. Eliot had even read a book. It was a new one that he had found in the library about UFOs. The book was interesting. It was writing about it that Eliot found boring. Still, he didn't think he could count on the homework ghost to write a book report. If he didn't know the nine times table, he might not know anything about UFOs either. Eliot decided that he had better write his own report.

On Friday morning Eliot handed in his book report. It had turned out to be almost two pages long because once he began writing about UFOs, there was a lot he had to say about them. Eliot sat down at his desk and pulled out his loose-leaf ring binder. Would there be notes waiting for him today? He could hardly wait to see. Inside the front cover was his first blue note from yesterday. Underneath Eliot's question, in very small print, were the words: *Of course I'm not a kid in this class.*

On the second note was written, *Don't do your home-*

work. See if I care. But someday, when it's too late, you'll be sorry.

And on the third note, the one on which Eliot had written "Can I meet you? What do you look like?" were the words *You have met me but you don't recognize me.* That one really stopped Eliot for a moment. What did it mean? When had he ever met the genie or the ghost or whatever without recognizing him? Was it invisible and he had looked right through it? Was the ghost in the room and looking at him right now?

Then Eliot remembered he had left one more note. He turned the pages, trying to locate it. Finally he found it. It was the note that said, "Don't you know the nine times table? Are you stupid or something?" On the note was written, *The stupid one is you—relying on some unknown, unreliable source for all your answers. Trust your brain. And don't be afraid to do a little work.*

"What are all those little papers in your notebook?" asked Grace Ann, leaning across her desk and pointing to the blue note that Eliot was reading.

"Just some stupid messages," Eliot said, slamming his notebook shut.

"Let me see?" she asked.

"No," said Eliot. He was lucky that it was time for music. The class lined up to go to the music room. They were learning about different famous composers and today they were going to hear music by a man named Schubert. Mr. North put a record on the phonograph and the students sat listening. But there was no way that Eliot could concentrate on music. He was too busy thinking about the little yellow and the little blue notes. Who had put the yellow ones in his notebook and who had answered the messages he had written on the little blue ones? Who had said he was stupid?

For all his reading about mysterious events and creatures, Eliot had never really believed in the supernatural. Now he wasn't sure what he should believe. Why didn't the message writer leave him messages at home? Why were the messages only about schoolwork? His room was a mess at home and his parents were always nagging him about cleaning it up. How come the ghost didn't care about that? Did the ghost live in the school building? For a fleeting moment Eliot wondered if Mrs. Wheatley could be the one leaving him notes. But that didn't make sense. No teacher would do a kid's homework for him. And Mrs. Wheatley certainly knew the nine times table. She wouldn't get any of them wrong.

Mrs. Wheatley never gave any homework over the weekend. But on the following Monday, Eliot took his books home. He didn't want to leave them around for that mysterious note writer to leave him any new messages. Where did it get off saying he was stupid? At home Eliot sat down and did his homework right away.

Mrs. Parks wasn't stupid either. She didn't comment on the unusual sight of seeing her son working so intently on his homework.

As for Eliot, he was amazed to see that the homework ghost had been right. Even going over all his answers to be sure there were no careless errors, he was done in under fifteen minutes. The ghost had said it only took ten minutes, but the ghost had made mistakes.

So there was still plenty of time for Eliot to go outdoors

and play with his friends. Having done his own homework, Eliot wasn't expecting any mysterious messages on Tuesday morning. But after lunch, while he was turning pages in his loose-leaf book, he discovered another yellow note stuck on one of the pages. He was sure it hadn't been there in the morning. The note said, *I'll still be watching you, but I think you can manage on your own. You're much too smart to be stupid. Don't forget—the choice is yours.*

"What does that note say?" asked Grace Ann when she saw Eliot studying the little paper in his notebook.

"It says mind your own business," said Eliot, and he banged his notebook shut. Then he felt a little sorry that he had said it. He was lucky to sit next to Grace Ann. Except for chewing on her hair, she was the best-looking girl in all of fifth grade.

Eliot looked around the room. Mrs. Wheatley had her back to him as she wrote on the board. His classmates were busy pulling out their notebooks and copying the teacher's words. None of them looked suspicious. Eliot turned his head upward toward the ceiling. Didn't ghosts float overhead? There was nothing above him but the white ceiling and the fluorescent light. There was no ghost looking down at him. Well, he hadn't really expected that.

"Eliot," called out Mrs. Wheatley, "you're supposed to be copying from the board. Not studying the ceiling."

A few of the students, including Grace Ann, giggled at the teacher's remark.

Eliot looked at Mrs. Wheatley. Then he shrugged his shoulders and began copying. He'd do his work now, he thought. But one of these days he'd catch that ghostly note writer in action. In the meantime he thought he might leave a note secretly in Grace Ann Connolly's notebook. He thought he'd tell her, *Stop chewing on your hair. Do you want to choke to death or something?*

About Johanna Hurwitz

When I was growing up, in a part of New York City called The Bronx, I never worried about the supernatural. I was a down-to-earth kid and didn't believe in anything unless I saw it myself. The Bronx Zoo is a famous place but even the scariest-looking animals I saw there were safely behind cages. So I wasn't afraid. However, my friend Rose believed in everything. She tried to convince me of the existence of magic. She believed in witches, ghosts, goblins, zombies, spooks, bogeymen, and all sorts of other fantastic creatures. When Rose talked about them, I almost began to see them myself. Perhaps I was wrong and she was right.

Since I'm not a hundred percent sure about whether or not there is a supernatural world out there, I generally write about what I do know: ordinary, everyday kids of the sort that I used to be and that you are now. I write about school days (*Class Clown, Teacher's Pet*) and summer vacations (*School's Out, Aldo Ice Cream*), about making friends (*The Hot and Cold Summer, New Neighbors for Nora*), and growing up (*The Law of Gravity, Hurricane Elaine*). But I've discovered that sometimes in life something happens that I cannot explain. David Bernstein in my book *The Adventures of Ali Baba Bernstein* would like nothing better than to meet a ghost in person. Although he hasn't yet met a ghost, he has come face-to-face with Santa Claus.

In my story "The Fifth-Grade Ghost" Eliot discovers something mysterious happening in his classroom. Perhaps someone is playing a trick on him. Perhaps these are human messages and not magic at all. Or maybe there is a ghost haunting his classroom. Who knows?

A hundred and fifty years ago a very famous writer of mystery and ghost stories, Edgar Allan Poe, lived for a time in The

Bronx. Today his old home is a museum. Perhaps his ghost visits there along with the tourists. Edgar Allan Poe seemed to know all about ghosts. And so did my friend Rose. I'm still trying to find out for myself.

*Emma Jean's dream comes true—
or close enough. . . .*

Eṃṃa Jean's Ghost

JOAN LOWERY NIXON

*A*S EMMA Jean neared the rusty arch that spanned the
entrance to the trailer park, she hugged her books
tightly and walked a little faster along the narrow path that
snaked through dust-covered clumps of sea grass. That
mean-eyed, snotty-nosed Roy Ludley from her sixth-grade
class was following her again, and she tensed, waiting for
his taunts.

"Ugly old Emma Jean Mailer lives in a rusty trailer," he
yelled.

Emma Jean twisted, shouting, "Get lost!" but she
tripped over a rut in the path and dropped to her hands
and knees, her books landing in the dust.

Roy laughed so hard, he bent double, while Emma Jean
scrambled to her feet and snatched up her books. Ignoring
his chants she ran under the arch and down the road to

146

the trailer her mom had rented while she tried to find a steady job as a waitress in this off-season seaside town.

Emma Jean unlocked the door of the trailer and slammed her books on the chipped dinette table. Always moving, always hoping for something better, Mom went from one waitress job to another, and Emma Jean hated it. She hated changing schools in midterm. She hated the kids who didn't want to make friends. Most of all, she hated the Roy Ludleys who made fun of her.

Sometimes she dreamed that one day she and Mom would live in a house with a green lawn and lots of flowers next to neighbors who didn't pack up and leave in the middle of the night. Grandma was part of her dreams—the warm, cuddling grandmother she could scarcely remember.

But Emma Jean knew there would never be a beautiful house or kids who were eager to be friends, and years ago Grandma had died. Dreams were only dreams, and they didn't come true.

Emma Jean's routine was to do her homework, then start supper; but instead, she slammed from the trailer and ran toward the beach, sliding and scrambling down a low embankment into a small cove eroded from the hill and sheltered from the cold sea winds.

Late-afternoon winter mists had already begun to creep in from the sea, and they fogged the cove, wrapping her in a damp, protective blanket. She tugged her sweater tightly around her as she sank to the sand, laid her head against her bent knees, and cried loud and angry tears.

Emma Jean could remember a time when she had been happy. She'd been very young, and Mom's smile was bright, and Grandma's lap was soft. "Oh, Grandma, Grandma," she cried aloud. "Why did you leave me?"

"I'm right here, Lovey." It was a voice soft as the mists, and for a moment Emma Jean thought she had imagined it. But she lifted her head and saw across the little cove a rounded, white-haired woman seated on a boulder. The hem of the woman's faded cotton print dress trailed across worn sneakers, but her eyes glittered with excitement, and her smile shimmered through the mists.

"Grandma?" Emma Jean whispered, prickles racing up and down her backbone. "Is it really you, Grandma?"

"You called me, and I came," Grandma said. "I've been waiting for you to need me. I always hoped you'd know that all you had to do was ask, and I'd be here, Lovey."

Lovey? There had been so many pet names. Vaguely, Emma Jean remembered *Lovey.* People were supposed to be afraid of ghosts, she thought, but how could she be afraid of her own grandmother? Warmth chased away the prickles, and she cried, "Oh, Grandma, I've missed you so much!"

"I've missed you too," Grandma said. "Sometimes I think about the baby games we played and how I used to hold you on my lap and sing to you."

"I remember," Emma Jean murmured, comforted by the memory of lullabies.

"How is your mother?" Grandma asked. "It's been such a long time. Is she well? Is she still just as pretty?"

"I—I guess," Emma Jean said, surprised because Mom always seemed tired and worried, and she wasn't used to thinking of her mother as pretty.

"And you, Lovey, are you happy?" Grandma asked with such wistfulness that Emma Jean was tempted to lie.

But she answered, "Not really. I'm lonesome, Grandma. Sometimes there are people who are mean, and I wish . . . I wish so hard I had a friend—a real friend I could have for keeps."

"Don't worry about mean people," Grandma said. "They're their own worst problem." She smiled again. "And you do have a friend. I'm your friend, Lovey. You'll have me for keeps."

"Even though . . . ? I mean . . ." Emma Jean blurted out, "Grandma, there's so much I don't understand about why we're here together and about ghosts and what they can do. Could we talk about what it's like to be . . . dead?"

Through the fading light and heavy mists Emma Jean could see Grandma shudder. "No," she said as she twisted her hands together. "That's not something I want to talk about."

Embarrassed at having disturbed her grandmother, Emma Jean bent over and began to draw circles in the cold sand. She wanted to apologize, but it was hard to find the right words to say. Finally she mumbled, "I'm sorry, Grandma. I don't know the rules, and I just wondered how you got to be here or why they let you come, or why you didn't come sooner. I don't know anything about ghosts. I just know I'm not afraid, and I'm awfully glad you're here, Grandma."

When there was no response Emma Jean sat up. The boulder across the cove was empty. She jumped to her feet, crying out when she realized Grandma had gone. Was it what she had said about ghosts that had sent her away?

A sudden spill of dirt and sand showered Emma Jean's shoulder, and she leapt aside as Roy Ludley slid down the embankment, landing at her feet.

Laughing so hard he could hardly talk, Roy said, "You're so stupid! Talking to a ghost! That's the dumbest thing I ever heard in my life."

Emma Jean yelled, "Shut up, Roy! She was *my* ghost! You couldn't even see her!"

"See her? Everybody around here has seen her. She's a crazy old lady whose daughter and granddaughter got killed in a car wreck a long time ago, and she wanders up and down the beach looking for them." Roy pranced around the cove, cooing in a silly voice, "Oh, Grandma, Grandma! Oh, Lovey, Lovey!"

Emma Jean's fury lifted Roy off his feet as she grabbed him and shoved him against the embankment. His shoulders were thin and bony under her hands, and for an instant his eyes were wide with fear. "Leave me alone!" she shouted at him. "Don't you ever follow me again! If I ever see you around here you'll be sorry!"

Dropping Roy to the sand, Emma Jean climbed out of the cove and up the path to the trailer park. She flung herself on the lumpy built-in sofa that served as her bed and cried for her lost dream until there was nothing left but dry hiccups.

As she struggled to her feet she caught a glimpse in the mirror of her pale, dirt-streaked, swollen-eyed face. It looked like a ghost mask tossed out after Halloween.

Emma Jean Mailer . . . the ghost.

Well, why not? A grandma was a grandma. A friend was a friend. Did it matter who was real and who was not, or whose dream came true?

Emma Jean made it through the next day by working in class as hard as she could and occasionally piercing Roy Ludley with a stare so intent that he stayed as far away from her as he could get.

As soon as school was over Emma Jean hurried to the cove and waited. She waited a long time, watching the mists grow thicker and damper, until the sand whispered with soft, shuffling footsteps, and the woman appeared.

"Hi, Grandma," Emma Jean murmured. "It's me . . . Lovey."

About Joan Lowery Nixon

We all have our own private *ghosts,* and loneliness can be one of the most haunting ghosts of all. But ghosts can be dealt with, as Emma Jean discovered . . . as many of us have discovered. I like to write about ghosts, whether private ghosts or preternatural ghosts. Three of my mystery novels have won the Edgar Allan Poe Award for best juvenile mystery from Mystery Writers of America, and many of them have won state awards in which readers vote for the books.

*Is Jacob too old to believe
in ghosts?*

When Life Gives You Lemons

MARION DANE BAUER

J ACOB PULLED the sheet up to his nose and stared at the
light hovering in the corner of the room. Eerily blue.
Dim. Even wavering. But there. Definitely there.

He had seen it the night before, too, and the night
before that. The night before that he hadn't been in this
unpleasantly strange apartment in this old house that rattled and moaned in the dark. He had been in his real
bedroom in the house he had always lived in on the corner
of Fifty-first and Cedar. With both of his parents. And his
whole life laid out around him. And no strange lights
jittering in the corner of the room.

There was a rational explanation for the light, of course.
There had to be. It was cast by a streetlamp. Or it was a
reflection of one of the neon signs on a store across the
way. Or . . . He couldn't think of any other, but there
had to be one. He was twelve years old, too old to believe in

153

ghosts or fairies or goblins or anything else conjured up in stories to populate the night.

It was his parents' fault that he was lying here in this unfamiliar room, staring at a mysterious light. *Why?* he had asked them. *Why are you doing this to me?* But they had just looked sad—and resigned, as though they were the ones who were without a choice in the matter. Though, of course, all the choices were theirs. Or his mother's, really. *She* was the one who had moved out.

Jacob, they had decided, could spend every other weekend with his dad . . . and his dog . . . and his house . . . and his friends. Every other weekend! That left 313 days to be imprisoned here with whatever weird thing was dancing around in the corner of this crummy room every night.

The light seemed to be growing larger, moving closer too. Jacob pulled the sheet up to his nose, then scooted down until it covered his eyes as well. But after a few seconds he couldn't stand not knowing what was going on, so he inched back up again, just far enough to see.

The bluish glow had stopped at the foot of his bed, where it hovered about four and a half feet off the floor. There seemed to be a shape inside it, just the barest suggestion of features such as might be visible in a full moon.

But then the "moon" floated even closer, and the form grew more distinct. It was the head of a girl. With sweet, sad features and a mass of long, curling hair. And no body at all.

A sound came from Jacob's throat, as involuntary as a sneeze. "R-r-r-r-a-u-g," he said. His limbs were overcooked spaghetti, except for his fingers that still clutched the sheet to his chin in a viselike grip.

The girl, if a disconnected head can be said to be an entire girl, jolted at the sound. Until then she hadn't been looking in Jacob's direction, but now she spun around, quite literally, until after several revolutions she stopped, facing him. A sound escaped from her too. Something like, "L-l-m-f-f!" And then she disappeared, just switched off like a lamp, and was gone.

Jacob was left quivering, staring into total darkness, choking on his own breath. He might have leapt out of bed and bolted to his mother's room, but he was so disoriented that he wasn't sure which direction he should go or whether she would be in her room if he found it or, for that matter, if his bed was still supported by the creaking wood floor.

If heads, or at least *a* head, could come floating through the air at him, then maybe the world was less solid than he had supposed.

The light flickered again, from the other side of the room once more, and Jacob stared at it, helpless and hopeless as well. Maybe someone, some*thing,* had been sent to get rid of him, to get him out of the way. Maybe all the arguments he had half heard in the night had been about him, about who would have to be stuck with him. It made sense. If each of his parents wanted to start over, pretending that the marriage had never been, then he was the one thing standing in their way.

The light was taking on a shape again, but it wasn't a head this time. It was an arm. Just suspended there in the

155

air. Delicate. Slender. Not an arm to be afraid of if it hadn't been floating alone in space the way it was.

And then the face was there, too, suspended just above and slightly to one side of the arm, first the chin and mouth, then the nose, eyes, forehead, hair. It was a pretty face, but twisted into an expression of revulsion, even horror . . . and staring directly at him!

"Are you human?" he whispered.

He hardly expected to get an answer from a head floating in the air, but he needed to ask. To his astonishment, though, the head answered promptly, though in a voice that dripped scorn. "Of course I'm not human! Why would you think that?"

Jacob drew in a wavering breath. "What—what are you, then?"

"I'm a ghost. What do you think?" the girl replied. She spoke as though being a ghost were infinitely preferable to being human.

Jacob sat up, pressing his back against the head of the bed and clutching his pillow against his chest. He couldn't think of another thing to say. His tongue might have been glued to the roof of his mouth for all the good it was doing him. He just stared at the head, which stared back at him.

"You're one, aren't you?" the girl asked, finally breaking the heavy silence.

"One what?"

"A human being."

Jacob nodded. Should he have denied it? From the way she'd asked, he had a feeling that he should have.

A look of such extreme distaste gathered, again, in the girl's face that an embarrassed heat climbed his neck. He might have just confessed to something nasty. He had always thought it was humans who were supposed to be repulsed by ghosts! This one seemed to have gotten the whole thing turned around.

When she continued to stare, her expression unchanged, his embarrassment shifted to irritation, and the irritation swept away fear. "You must have been human once," he pointed out, reasonably enough. "Otherwise, how did you get to be a ghost?"

The girl flapped a disconnected hand in the air, dismissing the thought. "That was long ago. Long, long ago." But then she added, sounding disappointed, "So . . . you can see me?"

"See you? Of course. I can see your head and"—Jacob examined her intently; the hand had disappeared—"and sometimes a hand or arm."

"Just that?"

She seemed pleased, and Jacob nodded. "Just that," he confirmed, though he wasn't sure that he wanted to say anything to please a floating head he had distinctly *not* invited to share his room.

The head jiggled, as though the invisible body were dancing in place. "Then I'm on my way," she said. Two hands appeared this time, clapping soundlessly. "I'm letting go like they said I should."

Jacob thought of asking who *they* might be, but he decided against it. She was talking about other ghosts, no doubt, and if there were others around here, he didn't want to know about them. One ghost, "on her way" or not, was as much as he was ready to cope with. So he asked instead, "What's so terrible about being human, anyway?"

157

"Humans hurt each other," she replied without the slightest hesitation.

Jacob considered arguing the point. *Humans don't always hurt each other,* he could have said. But there was something about the girl's face, a darkness behind the eyes, a twist to the mouth, that told him someone had hurt her. Besides, he had a sudden vision of his parents leaning toward one another across the dining room table, their faces clenched, which made him doubt his own argument.

"Is there anything I can do?" he asked instead. "To help you go, I mean?" If the girl wanted to leave, he was willing to help with that.

"No. Nothing. They say I've got to do it for myself." She sighed, a soft little hiss like a deflating balloon, and the blue light that seemed to form what substance he could see flickered. " 'Let go,' they say. 'Move on.' As if I'm not trying." She shrugged. He couldn't have said how he knew that was what she had done, since he could see nothing now but her face and her floating hair. But she pursed her lips, looked away, and somehow he sensed rather than saw the despairing lift and fall of her shoulders. "Until I can," she added, "I have to stay around . . . and watch."

"Watch what?"

"Humans. I'm told that they can be kind."

"I see," Jacob said, though he didn't really. He was already thinking intently of something else. It was something his dad had said to him the day Jacob and his mom had moved into the apartment. *When life gives you lemons,* he had said, squeezing Jacob's shoulder a bit harder than was entirely necessary, *make lemonade.* Well, life had certainly given him lemons lately, including a room occupied by a ghost, but until this moment he hadn't even considered what he might make out of it.

Maybe this ghost, whoever she was, was just another lemon . . . and it was up to him to make something out of having her here.

His mother had been awfully nervous since they had come here, locking doors, warning him about going outside after dark. It wasn't the best neighborhood, she kept reminding him. It was just the best they could afford for now. It would scare her for sure if she knew that she was locking herself, both of them, *inside* the apartment with this spook!

Maybe if she knew that she would decide that the world wasn't safe for a woman and a kid alone. Maybe she'd even be scared enough to go back home, back to his father. Maybe . . .

"Listen," he said to the girl. "I'm sorry I can't help you. I really am. But there's something you can do for me. If you're willing, that is."

"What?" The girl looked cautious.

"Just don't move. And don't disappear. I need you to stay right here."

"But you don't understand." She was shaking her head, the mass of light-struck hair swirling about. "I'm trying to leave this place. It's what I want more than anything, to be able to go."

"Oh, I don't mean forever. I mean just for a few minutes. Not even as long as you've already been here talking to me."

She stopped shaking her head, but she was still obviously uneasy.

"It'll be okay," he promised. "I just want my mother to
. . . meet you."

Her face relaxed a little. Her eyes grew lighter. "Your
mother? You've got a mother? Is she nice?"

"Yes, of course," he replied, impatient to get on with his
plan. "She's very nice. But she's never met a ghost. Not in
her whole life. And I want her to have a chance to meet you
. . . before you go away for good."

"Oh." The girl actually smiled. "Well! I suppose I
wouldn't mind meeting your mother."

"But she sleeps hard, you know," Jacob continued. "So
I'm going to have to yell pretty loud to wake her up. You
won't mind that, will you?"

"I won't mind," the girl promised.

"Okay. Then get ready." And Jacob settled himself back
into the bed, pulled the sheet up, and took a deep breath.
"Help! Mom! Mom! Help!" he called at the top of his lungs.

The girl's eyes widened, but he put a finger to his lips
and smiled, indicating it was all a joke. And then he sat up
to call again, "Mom! Help! Please, come!"

Footsteps in the hall. Running, though there weren't
more than a few feet between his mother's door and his.
Then the door flew open and the light in his room blazed.

His mother stopped in the doorway for an instant, tying
the belt of a faded blue robe. It was the same robe she had
worn for as long as Jacob could remember. Her short, soft
hair stood around her face like a dark halo. Then she was
at his side, bending over him, her hand warm on his arm.
"What is it, Jacob? What's wrong?"

"It was a ghost . . . a ghost! I saw it," he cried, forcing
tears. It wasn't so hard to do, really. "A floating head. Right

there. At the end of my bed." And turning away as though he couldn't bear to see it again, he pointed to the place where he had last seen the girl.

His mother straightened, and there was a moment's silence before she spoke. Her hand sought out his arm again. "But sweetheart, there's nothing there. You can see for yourself. It was just a bad dream."

Nothing? Jacob struggled to sit up, pulling himself free of his mother's comforting grasp. He stared at the empty spot near the end of his bed, then all around the room. She was right. There was nothing to be seen except for the walls of his new bedroom, his familiar bookshelf and dresser, a baseball glove and a hockey stick and a couple of unpacked boxes in the corner of the room.

The girl had promised to stay, though. She had promised!

Then he realized. With the room flooded with light, how could either of them see a being who seemed to be made out of light? All he had to do was to get his mother to flick off the wall switch, and then she would see the floating head. She'd never feel safe on her own again! Why, she'd probably start packing tonight to go home.

"Would you . . ." he began, looking directly into his mother's face.

"Yes, dear?" Her eyes were puffy with sleep and there were creases across one cheek from her pillow, but she managed a smile. The smile stopped him. There was something in it that he'd been seeing, and trying not to see, for the past couple of days. In all the exhaustion of moving, of settling into this apartment (an apartment that wasn't half, not even a third, as nice as their house), his mother had been looking tired and worried and scared. But there clearly was something more. Something that was harder to name. Did she look relieved too? Expectant? Hopeful?

If he scared her into going back, would her face shut down again? His father's, too, for that matter? Was that what he wanted for himself, to live with two people who didn't seem to be able to be in the same room without hurting one another?

"You're right," he said, sinking back into the bed. "It was just a dream. It couldn't have been anything else."

His mother smiled at him. "It must have been a whopper," she said.

"It was," he agreed.

She hesitated then, her hand fluttering just above him in the air as though she wanted to touch him again but wasn't sure she dared. Her hand found its way into the pocket of her robe before she finally spoke. "Jacob, I'm awfully glad you're here."

Jacob nodded. He knew she was.

She moved away then, but turned back at the door. "I know it's hard. But it'll get better. I promise."

He nodded again, and she reached for the light switch.

"No!" he said sharply. And when she gave him a questioning look, he added, more gently, "I'll turn it off. I just want it on for a few minutes."

"All right," she answered. And then she closed the door, and her bare feet padded softly across the hall.

Jacob waited until he heard her door close, her light click off, her bedsprings squeak, before he sat up to reach for the wall switch.

When the darkness descended again, he gazed about the

room. His mother had been right. There was still nothing to see, nothing at all. Had he frightened the girl away with all his commotion? Well—he lay back again—if he had, she would return. She would have to, probably. But maybe, just maybe, he wouldn't see her again. Maybe she'd seen something tonight that would make it possible for her to let go.

There was so much he hadn't asked the girl. When had she lived? Had she grown up in this old house? And who was it that had hurt her? Why, he hadn't even thought to ask her name!

Jacob turned his head slowly from side to side, feeling the softness of the pillow rise up to meet him, support him.

It'll get better. I promise, his mother had said. And maybe it actually would.

Tomorrow he would ask her if he could make some lemonade. The real stuff. The kind you made when you had lemons.

About Marion Dane Bauer

I grew up with my head full of stories. I was born in 1938 in the cement-mill housing at the edge of a small town in Illinois. We were surrounded by the enormous, dusty mill on one side, a cornfield on the other, deep woods and the Vermillion River Valley on the other.

There were rarely other children for me to play with, so I read, of course. But mostly I made up my own stories. I made up stories as I explored the woods or hiked through the rustling corn stalks. I gathered dolls or marbles or "ladies" made from hollyhock blooms and used them as characters in more stories. And when I happened to have a friend at hand, I told stories that we both acted out.

Becoming an adult changed only one thing. Now I write my stories down. My first novel, *Shelter from the Wind,* was an American Library Association Notable Book. *Rain of Fire* won the Jane Addams Award. *On My Honor* was a Newbery Honor Book. *Face to Face* was a 1992 Children's Book of Distinction for *Hungry Mind Review,* and won a Minnesota Book Award.

What's Your Story? A Young Person's Guide to Writing Fiction and *Ghost Eye* are my most recent books. *A Taste of Smoke,* also a ghost story, will be out soon.

Do I believe in ghosts? Well, I've never met one. But I do believe, sincerely, in the kinds of questions ghost stories require us to ask. How are we meant to treat one another? What is the significance of death? What is the significance of life?

About David Gale

David Gale is an editor of books for children and young adults. He has been a book reviewer, a textbook editor, and a substitute teacher. He holds a master's degree in children's literature and the teaching of reading from New York University. He edited *Funny You Should Ask: The Delacorte Book of Original Humorous Short Stories*. Born in Philadelphia, David Gale lives in New York City.